# Hymns for the drowning

Christopher Cyrill was born in 1970. His first novel, *The Ganges and Its Tributaries* was published by McPhee Gribble/Penguin Books in 1993. It was shortlisted for both the NSW Premier's Award and the Victorian Premier's Award.

Christopher published his first poem at the age of seventeen and has subsequently published numerous stories, poems and essays within Australia and overseas. He has also written for radio. He is the father of one daughter, Emily.

# Hymns for the drowning

*Christopher Cyrill*

ALLEN & UNWIN

The author would like to thank the Eleanor Dark Foundation, the Varuna Writer's Centre and the Marten Bequest for assistance in the completion of this novel.

This novel is named HYMNS FOR THE DROWNING in honour of the saint-poet Nammāḻvār. His book of poems for Vishnu was translated from Tamil by the poet and scholar A.K. Ramanajun. First published by Princeton University Press 1981 and subsequently by Penguin Books India, 1993. Ramanajun's book was first called *Hymns For The Drowning*.

Copyright © Christopher Cyrill 1999

All rights reserved. No part of this book may be reproduced or transmitted in any form or by any means, electronic or mechanical, including photocopying, recording or by any information storage and retrieval system, without prior permission in writing from the publisher.

First published in 1999
Allen & Unwin
9 Atchison Street, St Leonards NSW 1590 Australia
Phone: (61 2) 8425 0100
Fax:     (61 2) 9906 2218
E-mail: frontdesk@allen-unwin.com.au
Web:    http://www.allen-unwin.com.au

National Library of Australia
Cataloguing-in-Publication entry:

Cyrill, Christopher.
    Hymns for the drowning.

    ISBN 1 86508 043 8.

    I. Title.

    A823.3

Set in 10/15 pt Palatino by Bookhouse Digital, Sydney
Printed and bound by Australian Print Group, Maryborough, Victoria

10 9 8 7 6 5 4 3 2 1

*For Francis and Agnes,
Joseph and Edith*

So, the world happens twice—
once what we see it as;
second it legends itself
deep, the way it is.

William Stafford

*λ Capricorn divides   The equator snaps like the string of a guitar λ*

φ

Every winter, on the 24th of August, the citizens of my city celebrate Adamsday. It is a festival indigenous to our city, named after Adam Gordon who according to legend arrived at our shores after a shipwreck from the City of Fogs. In league with a tribe of the native population our founding father built a town of straw and daub huts in the place where our city square is now located. After years of cooperation and friendship, Gordon offended the ancestral spirit of the tribe and was killed by a ritual throwing of spears. His body was then taken and returned to the water he had emerged from. In some legends Gordon's body was impaled on an apple tree and therefore he wears in our recreation a crown of appleseeds. In another version of the legend he was stoned to death as he fled to the sea. This is also recorded in our festival, symbolised by the throwing of dried corn and parcels of dye. His offence to the ancestral spirit of place is ill defined. Early scholars of the indigenous people claimed that Gordon built a well on burial ground and was therefore seen as a thief of the dead, whilst more recent evidence suggests that Gordon was stoned for being a homosexual. Radical, contemporary scholars have claimed that Gordon never existed, that he was an amalgam of all the visitors who came with liquor and guns to trade or fight with the native population, and that Gordon's crucifixion is in fact a legend empowering the tribe and rejecting civilisation. For the citizens of my city it was the excuse for a parade.

Every year the civic fathers sponsor floats which are drawn down Brahe Street and past the library of my quarter on the way to the sea. The route is eight kilometres long and a straw Adam wearing an appleseed crown leads the procession. Revellers line the streets armed with satchels of dye and corn, confetti and riceballs. Sometimes even cans of beer and golfballs are thrown, although the crowd on previous parades has subdued violent behaviour. Not only is Adam pelted, the gods that follow in procession are tarnished and streaked with colour by the time they reach the sea. The men and women who pull the floats, the city band, even the mayor and the towncrier astride donkeys, are all besmirched by the time they reach the water, taking their soft punishments with goodheart. Only the native dancers from Caelum escape the crowd's mirth, for they come last in the parade, and their dance is sacred.

Throughout my childhood my aunt and I celebrated Adamsday with Archer, a family friend. My grandfather called it a parade of heathens. Though he ate the mutton roast and potato pancakes my aunt made every August 24th, he avoided the parade and the pelting of Adam. Once he helped us prepare the riceballs, even soaked a few in saffron water or beetroot juice. I remember him weighing a purple ball in his hand, staring into the congealed mesh of grains and feigning a stilted throw. If his face appeared amongst the crowd of revellers, or if he followed us within shouting distance, I never saw him. I could never understand why he would forsake the opportunity to direct a throw at an enemy, forsake the pleasure of seeing Adam's head reeling on its last straw.

I have been in the employ of the city now for four months. I have been given 24-hour access to the library to assist me in my search. Although the library was completed a year ago, it was only officially opened by the mayor last April when he cut a blue ribbon and made a speech about the merits of reading and retold the legend that persists amongst the native people. The legend tells of the time, when drought had parched Hevel River, the bloodbird revealed the song enabling flight to Jol-Col, a village elder.

The legend tells that Jol-Col one day returned to his people from a search for fresh water. He asked for berries and over his meal he told of the song and the power of the song. The villagers had no word for human flight so Jol-Col mimed the story. When he flapped his arms and pointed to the sky the villagers presumed him snakebitten or insane from solitude. They tugged his grey beard and pulled his big ears. Finally, when he became enraged that the tribe should doubt his story, he summoned all his strength and witched the song of the bloodbird. He flew to another land. Looking down upon his doubting brothers and sisters he saw them drop their spears and their waterskins and raise their voices and their palms to him, imploring his return, imploring his forgiveness. For generations after Jol-Col's departure, the tribe searched for his secrets in the dirt and in the trees. They questioned the sun and birds of the sun and their questions remained unanswered and their feet never left the ground. Legend says the bloodbird never sang again.

The mayor claimed we readers would find the secret song of the bloodbird in this modern library and drew a further parallel between the flight of birds and the flight of readers' minds. The crowd clapped and the mayor raised his hand to the applause and the crowd entered the library.

I watched a cartoon called 'Birdman' when I was a child. Birdman had wings and wore a brass headpiece that made him look like a falcon. His torso and legs were muscular but his true strength relied upon the sun. Whenever he felt his strength failing him he flew towards the renewing sunlight. He then descended with the strength of forty men to fight evildoers. I seem to remember that his sidekick was an eagle. They may have lived in a cave lined with straw.

I arrived at the library on the morning of last Adamsday as the barricades were being put out on the street for the revellers, as men on ladders hung balloons and streamers from shop awnings. I made my way into the library and switched off the alarm by turning a key clockwise then anti-clockwise. I collected the calling cards of the security men and checked the times of their visits. The doors closed behind me. I punched the number 4444 into the keypad and the alarm armed itself.

It felt like dusk in the library. Outside the cleaners were sweeping the kerbs and the footpaths. Warning lights blinked unmanned around unlaid roads and border guards were exchanging clipboards and ticking boxes. The first trams were leaving depots. I imagined the drivers breathing steam from the brims of their coffee cups. I imagined bakers removing the first loaves of the morning, but in the library it felt like dusk.

On one wall of the library hangs an untitled tapestry. The tapestry was woven in the late eighteenth century by an anonymous artist. In the scene depicted by the artist a woman with braceleted arms stands beside a blue man. They stand at the confluence of rivers before a background of banana and oak trees. Above the treeline a turret with elaborate cornices is visible and the red evening light of the setting sun shines through a window of the turret.

When I first saw the tapestry I presumed the man to be a god, or at least the offspring of one divine parent, since no one in the world in which I write has blue skin. I further presumed that the woman, whose right palm is turned outward to the god, was in fact his lover, or would soon be his lover. The god seems to be staring at the woman's palm, his head tilted forward. The crest of feathers he wears upon his head is in the process of falling.

I spent many hours staring at the tapestry, trying to

glean from the architecture and the river foliage, from the dress and expressions of the couple, some clue that would reveal to me the names of the lovers, their story, and the country or city, the town or village where the meeting took place. Thinking back over all the folktales and fables, the legends and myths I had read or heard in my lifetime, I could neither recall the lovers nor guess at their location.

The blue god must have intrigued the mayor as well. Perhaps on the day that he opened the library he decided that this blue divine and his paramour, these threaded figures, should join our parade.

So it fell to me last Adamsday to continue my search for the blue god.

# Jive an' all

Your father was a wonderful dancer, jive an' all the latest steps, the twist. And he always danced with all the girls, never to leave out even the fat ones. But then that's how your papa knew where to find him. All the lights and the band and the girls and boys jigging and jiving and then your papa standing to one side like a cowboy baddie. The whole dance stopped like someone is turning off the clock and no one came to help your daddy because in those days all good dancers got one kind of a kicking or another, all of them up to mischief. Terrible, shocking to watch, you couldn't see his face for blood. Never to be seen again. Off the face of the earth he went and your mother crying with a mouth like a horseshoe. Then you came along. At least you were a boy, you were worth something.

ϕ

When I first began my search for the blue god I concentrated on four things; the nameless god and the lover, the confluence of rivers and the foliage of the riverbanks. I decided that I had stumbled into the story mid-plot, long after the shy, initial meetings, long after the first seduction. I imagined that the weaver had woven her scene—I was sure the weaver was a woman—at the beginning of the climax of the story.

I sorted through the catalogue and found dictionaries on folklore. I read essays on world religions where I hoped to chance upon some mention of this blue divine and his paramour. I sought out fables of rivers to learn of the dramas that occurred upon their banks, to find some reference to the god whose colour mirrored the river he stood beside. It occurred to me that the god I sought was in all probability a god of rivers, perhaps even the spirit of the river itself. Perhaps he had assumed human form to pursue the bather around whose body he coiled during her nightly ablutions.

I turned page after page in reference books, sitting in a hidden corner of the library, walled in by dictionaries of myths and encyclopedias. I found illustrations of gods as animals, as landscape. Gods squatted in the corners of pages, gods mirrored other gods on disparate continents, and common amongst the myths and legends of many countries and written into the scriptures of many religions were stories of flood and exile, the parting of waters or the crossing of waters by foot.

I pored over an atlas to study the meetings of rivers and moved through maps of ancient civilisations, tracing the course of waters with my fingernail through Tiberias and Lagoah. I decided to seek those confluences within the lines of Capricorn and Cancer, knowing that banana trees could flourish only in close proximity to the equator. I flicked quickly through maps of continents, ignoring the Volga and Don, the Arkansas and Mississippi, becoming impatient with the Lands of the Midnight Sun.

The first object of my search was his name and yet, it seemed, I required his name to begin. For some reason I had assumed that the god and his lover had lived in a time long before Adam Gordon had reached our shore.

When I look at a map of my city, I draw in my mind a line from the church to the library and then from the library to my grandfather's home and then from home to the church. Though I have travelled on school and family excursions into the Rheita Valley and spent one summer fishing at the source of Hevel River with my grandfather, I feel as if I have never left this triangle, just as it seems I once lived always within arm's distance of my aunt, my grandfather and Archer.

I landed with my grandfather and Aunt Ida on the concrete shores of this city when I was four years old. We arrived by ship because my aunt is afraid of flying. I have few memories of the country I left. My grandfather called it the Old Country and forbade talk of it in our home. I remember mountains of turmeric and paprika at a hawker's stall. I remember a street where candles and incense burned before every door. I remember the sound of many men running over a flat piece of earth. I have other, impossible memories. I remember my mother breaking her ankle when she was nine years old. I remember the smell of a burning corpse. I secretly questioned my aunt about them and she told me of family legends and claimed that my blood's colour had a taint of all the lives that had led to mine, yet a taint so diluted not she, not her grandmother could name its true source.

I began to wonder if I had memorised the images that came into my mind when my aunt told me stories about my mother, or whether I inherited them. I prefer to believe that at my grandfather's death he willed to me the stories he had withheld from me in life.

I lived with my grandfather Joseph Manu and my Aunt Ida until I was twenty years old. We lived in a court, which on the city map looks like a tear. Behind our home on McCarthy Street was an alley where I used to play as a child. The alley is flanked by gutters and on days of heavy rain my grandfather would make me paper boats with foil hulls and paper sails secured with matchsticks. He would stand above me holding an umbrella as I raced the boats down the flooded gutters. At night I was too scared to walk along the alley alone, and lying down to sleep I often heard the gate to the alley being opened and heard men fighting with the broken bottles that I found there during the day. I now know that the sounds I heard from the alley were sounds from an alley in a dream.

My grandfather died two years ago and for the last two years of his life he rarely spoke. The last words I heard him say were words from his native language muttered in his sleep.

My grandfather's silence deprived me of more than affectionate words and knowledge. I felt uncomfortable near him. Although he had in my childhood taught me to play pen hockey and taken me on trips in his Gemini, allowing me to fly my balsawood plane out of the car window, he had never hugged or kissed me. Then, when he withdrew his words from me, I felt ashamed of whatever I had done to provoke his silence. I quickly learnt, after my aunt announced that Papa would no longer speak, to stop pestering him with questions. I never again asked him for help or retold him stories. My aunt continued to talk to him, to ask and answer the questions he ignored, and Archer often seemed to be talking solely to himself and remained unperturbed. Archer said that sometimes men ran out of words.

I learnt to understand the expressions on my grandfather's face. I learnt to recognise the frown that withheld laughter, that his nostrils could flare with interest or narrow with sympathy. He tugged his ears when he became angry with my aunt and she too recognised this sign for she ceased her bait and chatter. My grandfather had another face which I sometimes see in dreams. It is a face so expressionless he seems beyond any feeling available in this world. It is a face remarkable for its veil of dispassion.

Towards the end of his life my grandfather and I would spend every Sunday morning together in silence. He would wake earlier than my aunt and I and walk to the nearby deli where fresh loaves and sweetbuns were left on the doorstep. The deli, called Macquarie's Last Stand, would still be closed so my grandfather would choose the bread and buns he wanted and leave a note for the owner with our address and his choices. He returned later in the day to pay his debt. When my grandfather arrived home he would walk into my room and wake me by touching my foot. While I brushed my teeth and washed my face he would brew coffee. The stovecoil fire had burnt the base of his coffee pot in the shape of waves and by certain light these waves seemed crested with blue, as if the burns still retained the potential or memory of fire. I would sit down at the kitchen table, trying to resist the lure of icing and glaze until the coffee bubbled and drops hissed upon the stove. My grandfather poured two cups of coffee with milk and sugar and buttered the bread and buns. Then we sat and dipped our bread and buns in the coffee and ate. Drops of oil floated on the milky surface of the coffee and coffee dribbled down our chins from the soaked bread. We licked our fingers of icing and glaze and picked our teeth for the remnants of raisins. Then I would get up and he would nod his head without looking at me. By then the morning would have brightened and the dog awoken—I would see his muzzle raised at the kitchen window. I would return to bed and my grandfather would butter more bread and take it to the dog and duck, and wait for my aunt to awake and make him his usual breakfast.

Earlier this evening I sat on the footpath of a street named after a war and watched dark clouds drift past the spire of St Ambrose's Church. I took my clarinet from my case and fitted a reed and placed the shaft into the mouthpiece. I stretched my fingers. I fingered the keys and lay a blanket out in front of me. Before I played a note a passing man threw a few coins onto the blanket, as if he were paying for my daydreams.

I played a few notes on the clarinet. My fingers felt cold and stiff and the mouthpiece tasted of salt and smelt like smoke. I lay it back within its velvet case. I took a cigarette from its soft packet and lit it. I inhaled and exhaled. A girl with a long jaw entered a phone booth across the road and a group of men in black coats were standing outside a kosher butcher. Two young boys with sidelocks dangling to their shoulders were wrestling. A weathervane on the roof of the butcher turned slow circles in the wind.

When I first started playing the clarinet I dreamed of my family as troubadours, wandering over ancient hills and along young roads, stopping to offer a meal of beans and rice to a beggar. We owned a caravan which resembled the wagons used by pioneering families heading west to the wide plains of a country once known as the New World, and all our belongings and our dog and duck travelled with us. We were welcomed into noble houses and into the courtyards of kings, where I enchanted the princess with my clarinet and Archer dazzled the queen with his sleights of hand.

One night during a thunderstorm the dog was barking and banging at the kitchen door and the duck was running around the clothesline in circles. Archer went outside. He was wearing an orange jacket and light green pants and his face was deeply powdered. Mascara tears ran from his eyes. Rain began to wash his makeup off. Beneath the powder his skin was dark. He caught the dog by the collar and made him sit. The duck came and stood between his legs. Archer looked into the dog's eyes and began to sing. The dog whimpered and tried to escape his grip but Archer held it and continued singing. The thunder sounded but the dog seemed fixed on Archer and the song. It went down onto all fours. It rolled over on its stomach. In the rain and the thunder Archer sang to the dog and scratched its stomach until it fell asleep. He then caught the duck by the neck and pushed his thumb under its beak and looked into its eyes and it too fell asleep.

I picked up the coins from the blanket and looked up at the sky where the intersecting tramlines and phone cables looked like staves laid over the moon. I stamped out the cigarette and began walking home, past the church and library of my quarter.

The word 'quarter' which I use to describe the area in which I live is technically incorrect for my city has only two quarters, built one in front of the other. It is generally accepted that they are divided by Copernicus Street. I live in what has been nicknamed the Ambrose Quarter, the side of Copernicus further from the sea. Our neighbours refer to themselves as Anchors or Dockers. The people of both quarters are mainly immigrants. Words written in languages I have no knowledge of fade upon the walls of retail buildings and above the front doors of houses, advertising a ritual killing, I presume, or offering greetings and good passage.

I am writing these words on the balcony of the house I once shared with a woman who I knew as Mirren, a woman whose face I think of whenever I hear or read or write or remember the word 'love'. I began writing in this journal after Mirren disappeared, after I too decided upon silence, and though I know I am writing to remember her, I also recognise that I am writing the words I will no longer speak. Further, I write with the hope that the words once written will reveal to me a truth I could not previously understand or imagine.

I live two doors up from the library and from the balcony I can see through a window and into the foyer, where, each morning the rising sun casts a shadow in the pattern of a chessboard on the floor. Yesterday, as I stood within the second aisle of the fiction section of the library, I decided I would only borrow a novel that was written in the first person. For as long as I have been capable of reading I have understood that all the books of fiction on the shelves of personal and public libraries have been written by authors in this world, the world in which I now write. As a reader I understand that the novel I have borrowed or stolen, even if it is ghostwritten or plagiarised, has been handwritten or typed by an author in this world, a world where books are available on shelves for borrowers and thieves.

However, yesterday, as I stood in the aisle of novels, I began to wonder where in the world of its own fiction the book of the first person exists. When I read a novel written in the first person I understand that somewhere in the world of its own fiction the narrator has written a manuscript or told a story. Therefore, unless it is an oral tale, a manuscript exists and its pages are hidden somewhere within the pages of the novel. I am curious as to how the novel becomes available to me and as to its whereabouts, since, if it is available to other characters of the novel, it may be open to manipulation; names may be changed, observations and details influenced by criticism. I wonder what motivates the narrator, to whom or for what purpose the 'I' is writing, and, if the author does not allow their narrator to reveal these things to me, I presume myself a reader who exists only for a time in the world in which I read.

I chose a novel from the library shelves and sat down in the study section. I sat in front of a window divided into three rectangular panels, the same window I sat before last Adamsday. The window looked out onto the street along which the parade passed on its way to the beach of the Anchor Quarter. I began to read.

The narrator of the novel I was reading lived in the country in which I was born, while the author of the novel lived in the country where I now live. The narrator had once been in love with a woman whom he deserted because his family had arranged for him a marriage to another woman. The families of the bride and groom had come to this arrangement before the bride was born.

The author withheld from me the place where the narrator kept his manuscript. Therefore, though I remember my aunt telling me that I once played in the shadows of the novel's metaphoric temples and practised handwriting its native metaphoric alphabet, I felt exiled from my birthplace as I closed the book. However, I imagined that each day, while the narrator waited for passengers to ferry across the river, the narrator wrote on a small white pad the happenings of his life and he kept this pad in a metal box beneath one of the planks of his boat.

The day my grandfather left for the town of Morning, I stood at the kitchen window while my aunt fried kidneys and beans. My grandfather was packing a suitcase in his bedroom and every now and then he would walk into the kitchen, look for something in the fridge or one of the cupboards and then leave without having found it.

Normally my grandfather would sit at the kitchen table while my aunt made him breakfast. He would read the *Phoenix* newspaper until nine o'clock, after which he would throw the breakfast scraps to the dog and throw breadends and dried corn to the duck. Every morning, when my grandfather read the *Phoenix*, he would turn first to the public notices. As he read he would point to each word with his pen and when I read the paper after him I would find words underlined and misprints corrected.

When I turned finally to the public notices I would see encircled paragraphs thanking St Jude, helper of the helpless, which appeared almost daily between the announcement of lotto winners and photos of missing persons. Often I would also find encircled thankyou notices to St Anthony of Padua and the prayer to the Virgin Mary, the prayer never known to fail, which began 'O most beautiful flower of Mt Carmel', and which required the favoured to reprint or publicise the prayer.

In the weeks before my grandfather left, a paragraph appeared in the public notices for twenty-four consecutive days. The paragraph reported a sighting of a white-haloed woman above the confluence of the rivers Hevel and Schiller, witnessed by sixteen residents of the town of Morning. All of the witnesses were said to agree that the vision was neither a trick of the dusklight nor a chance formation of clouds but a true visitation by the Virgin. The paragraph concluded by calling for other devotees of the Virgin to join the vigil at the confluence of rivers on the first day of the next lunar month.

My grandfather walked out of his bedroom carrying two suitcases and a blanket. He walked out the front door and I heard the car boot shut. My aunt turned off the stove. The kidneys glistened with fat. Then she poured some lentils from a clay jar onto the table. She sat down and sorted the black and green lentils from the orange ones. She asked me to bring her a bowl of water and to turn on the pressure cooker. I took her the water as she swept the lentils into the shape of a crescent moon and then swept them into a bowl. She put a bay leaf into the bowl of water.

As my grandfather walked back into the room my aunt stood up, went to the fridge and took out a colander of okra, which she called ladies' fingers. She washed and drained the okra while my grandfather opened a cupboard from which he produced a metal box. He opened the box and drew out a jar of tiger balm with his thumb and forefinger and he uncapped the jar and rubbed a little balm in each hand and then he rubbed each of his elbows and the back of his neck. He recapped the jar and put it back into the box and then withdrew a red globe and peered at the filament and then he replaced the globe and closed the box and put the box under his arm.

My aunt sat down and sliced ladies' fingers into thin pentagons, the sap rising and falling with the quick knife like liquid thread. The pressure cooker began to whistle and my grandfather turned to leave. I waited for him to stop, to return for something he had forgotten. I heard the front door close.

I remember a postcard my grandfather showed me during our first year in the New Country. The postcard was a reproduction of an aerial photograph taken of a plain in an unknown country where the earth had re-emerged from beneath a covering of snow, in a pattern that resembled the face of Christ. At first I could see only patches of black and white. My grandfather told me to close my eyes and then to reopen them. He asked me what I saw and I said I saw a valley leading to a lake. He looked at the postcard again and cursed under his breath and turned the card over and outlined the face with his finger. He asked me again what I saw. I watched as a dark face came up from the snow and I said I saw Jesus.

The pressure cooker continued to whistle and my aunt lit a cigarette and inhaled and dusted ash into the bowl of soaking lentils.

## Clockwise

Some are liking the watching of a sweet fish in a bowl or pond for relaxing and others are all for dice and carrums but I like the watching of the clock. When I nursed the *butcha* I came into the habit of counting time to lull him toward sleep and so into this habit I came and now between two and three which is my hour for relaxing I stare at the pretty clock and the face going round but staying still with the seconds like eyelashes falling and my mind wanders back to the dances and Hadja Roy.

φ

As I wandered last Adamsday along the library aisles and as I leafed through books and ran my finger up and down indices searching for a clue to the name, or perhaps the name of the god itself, forgotten dreams resurfaced on my mind. Sometimes the memories came in waves and I remembered the topography of cities and lovers whose bodies changed into mythical animals during the act of lovemaking. At other times, in my mind's eye, I saw only glimpses, coordinates to a lost map.

Once when I was a child I pressed my hands against my bedroom window and watched a bloodbird that had landed on the windowsill. The bloodbird pecked the pane. Its eyes were red and its feathers looked frayed. The next morning I heard pecking at the windowsill again. I pushed apart the curtains. The window was fogged up. My fingerprints remained from the night before, eight uneven ovals printed on the glass. The ovals reminded me of illustrations I had seen of the phases of the moon, the declinations and inclinations of the moon in orbit, revealing and withdrawing its face from the earth.

I imagine my memory as a sea whose currents are controlled by a moon within my mind. I sometimes think of this moon orbiting my brain, rhythmically, seasonally, as if certain memories come only in winter. I imagine this moon drawing to the shore of my mind the memory of a vine trailed over a gravestone, the ripple of Mirren's thigh under the smack of its suspender.

Mirren made mosaics. She had a worktable set up in her room. On the table in old tomato tins, old apple tins she had sorted moonstones and pebbles, seashells and agates. She owned a chisel and hammer, pliers and various kinds of glues and cement. Her mosaics were often simple, stylised renderings of dogs and bears or rudimentary faces with seashell ears and eyes.

She worked by candlelight. Her worktable had a legend of candles of different kinds, of different lengths. Her father, she had once told me, was a candlemaker and she liked to imagine he was hovering nearby as she worked on her craft.

One night I sat with Mirren and watched her work. The candles were lit and the window to her room was open. A wind blew through the window and the wicks burned back into the wax and the light created flickering shadows across her face. She worked from a drawing of a woman carrying a vase and I could see from the drawing that she planned to hem the woman's dress in moonstones, and she had set aside two bright pink seashells for her eyes. As she soaked and dried tesserae she told me that her father had been a tall man with a dark red moustache but with his red hair dyed black. Candlemaking was his hobby but he made money from it. He sold his candles of beeswax or tallow, candles scented and carved with crosses to a craft store in the City of Legions. The money he made from candlemaking funded trips to the Black Country, where he worked mainly as a restorer of murals and frescos. Mirren said that if I were to travel to the Black Country I would see her father's favourite restoration, a mural of Christ at the Wedding of Canaan, restored from beneath a century of dust from the feet of penitents, from beneath a century of candlesmoke.

I looked at the candles on the table. The wind had caused the candles to burn unevenly. A build-up of wax had formed at the back of the tall white candles. The crusted wax resembled wings. The flames seemed like oval heads. The candles came to resemble angels with heads of fire.

## δ

Looking again at the tapestry I was reminded of the movies my aunt and Archer watched on Saturday afternoons, movies full of harem girls and gilded horses, bejewelled goblets and belly dancers whose coinbelts and shimmering veils seduced empires from kings or the heads from prophets. In fact, the sinuous carvings on the turret in the background of the tapestry reminded me of my aunt pointing at the screen in mute agitation whenever she heard the conniving plot of the treacherous queen or saw the rogue prince, dagger poised, lurking in the shadows of the temple walls. I recalled that the movies my aunt and Archer watched were often set in ancient times, amongst ancient people in empires approaching ruin. Often the cities where these movies were set no longer existed on maps of the modern world.

Aunt Ida and Archer argued throughout the movies, debating the suitability of lovers and the worthiness of kings, but they agreed that none of the movies produced by the City of Falling Stars could be compared favourably to their favourite movie *Hanif*. Years after my aunt told me the story of *Hanif* I was to learn that it was a remake of a movie made in the City of Falling Stars called *Harvey*. In *Harvey* a character played by James Stewart believed his best friend was an invisible six-foot rabbit. He bought Harvey drinks, discussed family matters with him. In the movie remade in the Old Country Hanif was a six-inch-high elephant whom only the character played by former bandleader Hadja Roy could see. Archer claimed the greatness of the movie lay in its singing and dancing. My aunt would rebut him by saying every movie had at least one catchy song or fashionable step and that Archer was more foolish than he looked, and indeed he looked like three kinds of foolish, for the performance of Hadja Roy, a man she had known, was what gave the movie truth.

My aunt collected matchboxes and postcards, statuettes and figurines. She displayed her keepsakes in a three-tiered glass cabinet which stood in the living room of our home and each month she would remove the statuettes of stone and plastic, the rubber farm animals and bronze buddhas, and then remove the tiers of glass and dust and wipe them down. In the following hours my aunt would rearrange her three-tiered world, placing and replacing porcelain giraffes around a blue cellophane pool, creating plastic farm scenes where wolves huddled under plane trees made out of cocktail umbrellas. Her lovers were often mismatched—porcelain ladies in the dress of the 1920s waited for tin knights on inch-high horses, a nurse Barbie bowed to accept a kiss from a cornflakes packet troll. Animals of marble, wood—even a matchstick elephant, trunk raised on the glass planes—stalked or fought each other, or fled north to the ends of the world from a fire made of tissue paper and tinsel. Buddhas laughed or reclined. Wooden monkeys did not hear or see or speak of the lapis sparrows, St Francis with the crooked eyes.

# Kiss

You must never kiss a woman on the forehead if you do not plan to marry her. You may kiss a man on the forehead if he is a good man and doesn't drink or smoke or go out gallivanting and be only good for four ways of spending money. And if you look like that I'll slap your bloody face. If not for me you'd be in the gutter. I think maybe you can kiss a priest on the forehead even if he drinks and smokes but not if he gambles in the temple. Lord *bayah* Christ, who is to be remembering, one day I'm making modaks for puja, next I have a seat in hell because I've made the modaks. And want to know the secrets why? Because your papa is touched in the head. One day he tries to make us more one half than the other, like we're two Tippi Headress daughters of his, thinking that way we'll be chummy chummy with the boys at his club. How mummy laughed when he thought he could swap.

ф

I picked up a book on the Hopi Indians and began to read. I saw an illustration in the book where a man wore a box zigzagged with blue and yellow lines upon his head. He was also wearing wings. A child sat at his feet. The man wearing the boxhead seemed to be circling the child, to be hunting him from a height.

I knew from previous reading of the Hopis that they celebrated festivals of the sun: the Soyal, the Niman Kachina. The village elders appointed skywatchers, men and women whose sole duty was to watch the stars for signs that the time of feasts and sacrifice approached. I had read of other tribes who once populated the plains surrounding the City of Magnificent Distances, whose tribesmen painted starcharts on buckskin bags so as to navigate long journeys. Often these bags held fragments of meteorites or wolf's tooth, sacred items considered vital for safe passage.

En route to the town of Morning my grandfather's Gemini skidded in the night rain and crashed through the barrier of a small wooden bridge on the outskirts of the town of Tucana. The police of my city surmised from the crash site that my grandfather was thrown through the windscreen of his car, the glass of which severed his hands. The accident occurred on a Friday evening, and over the weekend the downpour continued and caused the river to break its banks and the body to be carried away on the floodtide. The search began when the rain stopped and the floodwater subsided and the car was winched from the river and the river dragged. No body was recovered. My grandfather's hands were found by a young girl in a clump of milkweed some kilometres away.

I followed after first hearing of my grandfather's death his route to a destination he was never to reach on a map I looked up in the library. I followed the Russell Highway with my finger and came first to the town of Lyra and its twin town Ascella, then Tucana, then Caelum. My finger paused on the map midway between Tucana and Caelum.

Long before I saw the dancers of Caelum at my first Adamsday parade I had heard of them from people who had travelled far beyond my city, people who had travelled to towns so small that they became lost in the broader cartographies of state and country. I had heard that when the citizens of Caelum danced they were painted in ochre and their genitals were exposed to the audience. They were said to have danced on the streets the dances they perfected at their private feasts. They were said to have danced for rain and for the end of rain and to have danced for their old spirits and for crops.

I imagined that each of the towns my grandfather passed or would have passed through had within its borders a hotel or a hostel where a traveller could rest and take refreshment. I imagined my grandfather naming in his mind the familiar petrol stations and libraries. Yet I also imagined him passing mountains and deserts, rivers and valleys named in a language long dead even on the tongues of its native speakers and being startled by the ascension of birds and the flights of herds of animals he could not name. I imagined him feeling threatened by the quills and teeth of animals, the potential poisons of the land, and though I had nothing to fear for him I still felt afraid of the confusion he would have felt if he were still alive.

Many times since my grandfather's death I have crossed in sleep to a dream city. In the dream city I move through streets where the sun is rising, past people who seem ghostly in the morning light, towards a graveyard.

The first morning that I woke from this dream of travelling towards a graveyard in the dream city, I took the honey and the bread from my cupboard and as I prepared my breakfast I tried to recall in precise chronological order the progression of the dream itself. As I laid out my knife and plate and took the butter from the fridge I recalled descending the stairs of my house and walking out onto the street, where a boat suspended on a trolley and a bracket of wheels stood by the kerbside. Although the streets were different and the citizens of my dream were strangers to my waking hours, my home in each city was identical. As I spread butter on the bread, I recalled sliding my arms into a harness which towed the boat and trolley. I walked along a grey street full of ghostly people, pulling the tilted boat behind me. I seemed unremarkable to the workers and pedestrians keeping to the schedules of their day, and as I dipped the honeytwirl and drizzled the bread I passed the crossroads of a street named Biela and a street named Halley, passed a greengrocer with blue and yellow awnings, until I faced the green spiked fence of the graveyard. As I got up from the kitchen table and walked to the stove to brew coffee, I recalled opening the gates of the graveyard with an iron key. I pulled the boat along the cracked cement path of the graveyard.

As I took my first sip of coffee I recalled passing the Isabella Lawn on which a wall for cremation urns stood. Across the pathway there was a plaque to commemorate the unknown dead and those who died in the war.

The boat I pulled behind me was about three metres

long. It was strip-planked in redwood and its oars were spooned.

To my left and to my right were crypts and graves that dated from the 1890s to the present day. The earliest inscription was 1891, on the family crypt of the Greenlands, tailors and settlers who arrived in the capital in 1872 and whose youngest heir died childless in 1907. The headstone of the crypt was in the shape of an anchor.

The graveyard occupied a whole block of the dream city. I saw its topography in dreams of flight. The icons that remained were faceless. Between the high spiked fence sprouted the natural graffiti of weeds, flourishing in their green logic. Graves had collapsed under their own weight. Rain and wind had erased many of the names and the dates of the dead.

At one point in the dream I stood on my grandfather's grave. In a cameo on the face of the headstone there was a photograph of my grandfather in profile. Water had leaked into the cameo and marked his face with brown spots. The edges of the photograph had turned to mush. I looked around at the other tombs and crypts, the dark and light marble guarded by stone winged or hooded figures, granite holy books unfurling, and atop one grave a clay bell poised forever at the top of its arc. I saw the course and spread of milkweed and couch, ratshit in drains and in the gullies leading to drains, and lawns unraked or unsown.

I had my grandfather's walk. I sat like him, with my legs crossed at my ankles. I often still catch myself opening and closing my fists, as he did, when I become impatient with someone or with something. However, my dark skin, my aunt has told me, comes from my father and I have my mother's eyes. Once I sat down with my aunt's box of family photos and sorted through the pictures of my mother, my grandmother, through invitations to railway dances and a handful of old coins, hoping to find someone somewhere who bequeathed to me my talent for the clarinet. In hindsight perhaps I searched for some clue that I had inherited my father's talent for music.

My grandfather's father was a hunter. He had once killed a boar while lying flat on the ground. His father before him lived in the City of Fogs and helped design the train line that connected my mother's native city with many of the cities I had daydreamed as being the birthplace of my father.

I am the son of a man whose name I have been forbidden from hearing or, at least, has never been mentioned within earshot of me. Aunt Ida insisted that he was dead. My mother's name was Amba Manu. They met in the typing pool of Poran and Son Printers in the capital city of the Old Country. My father began leaving love notes on her desk. The notes were unsigned but my father was the only man working in the typing pool. In the notes my father promised my mother that he would find money for them to migrate. He described the house he would one day build for them both, the inside toilets and hot running water, and the fragrant gardens he would plant so that each season the east winds would bring a new bouquet to my mother's nose. He wrote of the wealth he would accrue by playing the stockmarket and selling his handmade paper door-to-door in the affluent cities of the New Country. He wrote also that if she allowed him to approach her father with the proposal of marriage he would waive the dowry that was owed to him.

My father fled the capital after my grandfather beat him with a hockey stick, and a week after my birth my mother died from an infection that came into her blood when a midwife washed her womb with unclean water. Bikh water, my aunt called it.

I preferred to believe my mother died of weariness. I believe that when she imagined the days of shame ahead and saw the disgust in my grandfather's eyes and watched him tugging his ears and bemoaning the loss of his good name and the name of his father before him, my mother became weary and allowed the illness to thrive. I never blamed her, imagining the gossip, the stones of her neighbours, and her life without the hope of her own home or the chance of a husband. In my mind I saw her slightly stooped over the typewriter, as she is in one photograph I have of her, the clock in the background frozen at eight to twelve, but she is fading. She alone withers within the constancy of film.

In my mind the branches of my family tree have come to resemble the streets of a city, a city founded by my furthest antecedents, a couple whose own parents, grandparents cannot be named. Therefore I can never find the true origins of my familial city, its streets extend to areas, to times I cannot imagine. The map I unfurl and smooth out in my daydreams is only a fragment, bordered by a no-man's-land where the streets of my forebears, Kulkarni and Jehosophat, O'Toole and Audrey, are covered by sand.

The court shaped like a tear in which the three of us lived had once housed a policeman and his dog. A legend of the court often told to new neighbours concerned one Adamsday when the dog attacked a child who had thrown stones at it. The policeman heard of the attack from the child's parents when he returned from his Adamsday duties. He leashed the dog and brought it out into the middle of the court and shot the dog dead.

Another legend popular amongst our neighbours told of the man who flew a flag on his front lawn. The flag was the national flag of a country that was renamed after a war. I have no knowledge of the country or the war that rewrote its boundaries but I was told that its former design incorporated stars and moons and the colours blue and white. Every Monday the man of unknown origins would hoist his flag and every Monday night someone would burn the flag down. The man became vigilant and asked for police help. He neither slept nor ate while keeping watch on his flag. He armed himself with knife and gun, with phone and megaphone. But neither he nor any curious neighbour saw the hand that lit the flag, though every neighbour saw the flames and heard the man's cries. The flag just seemed to self-ignite. The older tenants of the court claimed to have seen first-hand the flag burn down. Others touched their noses and said nothing or mimed the firing of an arrow. The man sold his house and moved away. He took his flagpole with him.

# The bride's halva

Your daddy had for a time a job working as a bricklayer making a post building. Part of his job meant he was to get the bricks from the kiln and for the getting of the bricks he had Bhima the elephant. Bhima could pull six or seven trays behind him and down Chandresekhar Street people would see Bhima coming gentle as a calf and get out of the road and someone might give him peanuts or corn for corn he loved.

Anyway Bhima thought he was half man and one girl used to spoil him and give him the good halva she should have kept for her own table and her name was Sarita. Your daddy had an eye for the ladies and more than an eye, the wastrel, but even he wouldn't go near Sarita because Bhima would get jealous and stamp his feet and blow his trunk like a trumpet and not work even if you pulled his ears and thumped his thick skin. So one day Sarita was getting married and was having her hands done and all, oh god what I forgot to say was that she had a big dowry and all, now I've missed my train of thinking. Anyway here comes Bhima running to stop the wedding. I don't know how he found out, maybe your wastrel father told him because he was always causing mischief. So here comes Bhima running and pulling a tray behind him blowing his horn and making a racket during the service, so much so that the groom's elephant took off in a panic. Not forgetting that the groom and his family were high caste and this was such a disgrace and the father of the groom had guests come all the way from overseas and one of the guests actually caught typhoid and was sealed off in a separate room and died one day not so long after the wedding with his wife threatening to court. Anyway here comes Bhima running and pulling a tray of bricks and making a noise until Sarita finally came to balm him and tell him that she loved him and would meet him in the next life and there she would marry only him. And so on her anniversary each year even when her husband took her off to a rich country, so I heard, she made a little halva and kept it to one side for Bhima and Bhima worked all his long life with the bricks. Though the post office was never built because your daddy stole some supplies and so if they built it his face would have been the first to go up there wanted.

ϕ

I restructured my search. I reasoned that the weaver, having set her lovers by the confluence of rivers, would certainly have chosen rivers famous for the civilisations founded on their banks and I further believed that only a civilisation of vitality and endurance could have produced the intricate architecture in the background of the tapestry. I felt assured that no nomadic tribe or barbaric horde would concern itself with monuments or temples.

I came by the rivers of Babylon to Sumer where the Tigris meets the Euphrates. I read of Lilith, a goddess with talons and feathered legs, and saw an illustration of the Moon god at Ur but I flicked past, for the woman in the tapestry bore no resemblance to Lilith, nor was the woman a goddess. She had dark skin. Her arms were long, as were her fingers. She wore flowers in her hair and led a peacock on a gold chain. She seemed remarkable to me because she had attracted a god only by the guile of her transient flesh.

I looked past the tropics and followed with my eyes the course of the Nile, consulting encyclopedias, cross-referencing. I drew my finger down past Thebes and Abydos, past Giza Akhenton and the Fayum Oasis. I saw in an atlas Memphis marked by a pink triangle in the Nile Delta and read of Menes, the founder of Memphis. The Ancient Egyptians believed Menes was the living embodiment of Horus, the falcon god. I imagined that Menes with his divine origins and perhaps even an inheritance of flight could easily be placed, at an hour approaching dusk, by the confluence of tributaries of the Nile. I imagined Menes with his head slightly bowed, anxious because his lover was late. Then I imagined the clinking of her bangles.

I found I could explain his need for secrecy. Certainly the conqueror of Lower Egypt would have arranged a marriage to inspire peace with a rival king or to lull the gods, but I had seen in those Sunday movies the lust of viziers for winebearers and the eyes of the dauphin come to rest upon the cleavage of a servant girl, and I knew that kings would risk even their empires for love or lust. Certainly, I reasoned, the prospect of war or the wrath of the gods would exile lovers to a covering beneath trees.

I felt close to the lovers while rifling through texts on Ancient Egypt, trying to match a lover with Menes from history or myth, as outside the library barricades were secured to the road with L-shaped clips and early children came to mime throws at the empty road.

A further hour into searching I saw Menes depicted in pots and stiles and I knew that I had been mistaken. Menes' headdress was of leather and cotton and he wore a sharp beard along his jaw. Furthermore, he was the colour of clay.

I recalled, however, that banana trees could survive in a temperate climate. My grandfather had once found the roots of a banana tree at the city tip and had brought the roots home and planted them in our neighbour's backyard. Our backyard was covered in concrete to simplify, my aunt argued, the cleaning up after the dog and duck.

My grandfather had long hair which he tied back in a loose plait with a strip of leather. I remember those times when he beat my aunt the plait would unravel and the veins in his biceps would twitch on the surface of the skin, as if caterpillars within his flesh had awoken. He hit her when she accused him of sleeping with the ayahs who lived with them in the Old Country and of hiring prostitutes when my grandmother went to stay in the house of the midwives. He beat her when she dropped food and he beat her when she drank gin. At other times my grandfather beat my aunt for my wrongdoings.

Whenever my aunt cried her head moved up and down, as if she were agreeing with the tears, and, on those nights when my grandfather took off his leather sandals and hit her arms and buttocks she would nod her head and press her palms against her eyes to stop the crying for he would beat her until the weeping ceased.

When the three of us lived together in the court shaped like a tear we lived beside a white house whose driveway was guarded by stone lions. The owner of the house was named Miss Carpetto. Her house always seemed full of voices and music, the sounds of glasses clinking and knives scraping against plates, but as far as I can recall she lived alone and rarely had visitors. Her backyard was full of plum trees and lemon trees, bordered with pots of rosemary and basil. Ferns hung from a trellis in baskets and grapevines ran along the west fence. With the help of my grandfather she planted a mango tree and a month later, again with his help, she planted the roots of the banana tree. The mango tree withered and died, but the banana tree flourished and littered the yards and eaves of her neighbours' houses with its leaves, and it bore tiny green inedible bananas which rotted in their skins.

Miss Carpetto's kitchen window was lined with figs and apples, lemons and plums preserved in glass jars. When I first began to notice within myself a desire to touch and kiss women, I would often imagine her feeding me whole plums, the syrup dripping over my lips, my tongue moving over her fingers.

Depending upon the season, baskets of fruit and bouquets of flowers would arrive on our front doorstep. I remember one of the fruits whose name I have never learnt had tough, crinkled skin with black seeds encased in its flesh. My grandfather would savour this fruit, dusting it with salt and finishing it in two bites. Often I would steal this fruit for him. Under the ruse of retrieving hockey or soccer balls I would jump Miss Carpetto's fence and pluck whatever fruit I could from her trees, occasionally even stealing an odd rose or sprig of hyacinth which I would give to my aunt, who, although discouraging me from theft, would call me a gentleman and kiss my cheeks.

Then, one day when I had jumped her fence to actually retrieve a hockey ball, I plucked a plum from a low bough and Miss Carpetto saw me. I presume she told my grandfather for that night my aunt was too sore to cook and her bruises were the colour of plums. Thereafter, every month or so, depending upon the season, a few tennis or hockey balls would come bouncing into our backyard. The baskets kept coming to our door but they contained only fallen fruit, or fruit on the point of turning.

Years later, in our city square, a juggler lost his rhythm and sent his set of balls bouncing between my feet and I felt responsible for his failure and the workings of gravity, and maudlin for a time in my life when a woman with sweet fingers lay fresh fruit at my door.

The word 'maudlin' is derived from the name Magdalene, specifically the biblical Mary Magdalene, the whore whose feet were washed by Christ, against whose body Christ challenged a mob to cast the first stone.

Only a decade ago it would have been blasphemous to say that Christ had been Magdalene's lover. To even imagine the meeting of their bodies would have been anathema or, to paraphrase my aunt, would have rotted your heart from the inside out. Nowadays, however, radical scholars of the Bible propose without ridicule that

Christ loved Magdalene with a love that approached desire. Though they debate as to whether this love was consummated, they agree that the Son of God felt lust as does any man. According to a city legend a sect who worships the child of Christ and Mary still practises its religion somewhere in the Altai mountains and I had contemplated whilst reading of walled cities and the garden of Gethsemane, Christ bathing her feet, her thighs, and a long kiss in the shadows of hanging palms, unseen and unrecorded by Matthew, Mark, Luke and John.

Whenever I was sick as a child my aunt would heal me with what I thought for many years was the sacred heart of Jesus. Above my grandfather's bedhead, on a wooden shelf covered in silk, stood a porcelain bust of Christ. Christ was surrounded by plastic Virgins and yellowing Easter cards, plastic roses and candles carved with the word 'INRI' or doves. In Christ's body, in the place of his heart, a red globe burned. The light of the globe was imperceptible during the day but at night it cast a red glow over the bedroom. It was a game of mine to approach the borders of the light, the edges of the room where the light ended. To step outside the light, I imagined as a child, was to enter a world where I was beyond the salvation of Christ.

During illness my aunt would shine a heat lamp upon the part of my body where I complained of pain. The heat lamp looked like a floodlight. It was dark red and stood on a tripod. I believed that my aunt had taken the heart of Jesus and put it into the lamp so as to save my life. The heat was at first comforting but soon began to burn. Sometimes I'd ask for the lamp to be turned away from my body and immediately I would imagine the infection returning. I would wait to see how close I could come to death before asking for the lamp to be redirected on me.

There is a trick to distinguish the sleeping from the dead whereby a mirror is held close to the mouth or nose: the living will leave an impression of breath on glass whereas the corpse will face unseeing their unclouded reflection. It occurred to me during my search that catching the impression of a dream is like catching the impression of breath left on glass; it is as if memory is breathed by another sleeper into my mind. It seems that just as the breath withdraws, after casting its shape of an unknowable continent, so does the glimpse of dream, and I seem exiled from that world or country, field or room where once I had been a traveller in a cloak of sleep. Yet, like any exile, I seem only a breath or sigh, a step or stumble away from my next homecoming.

## A bird's life

Sweetly, sweetly the bird comes to my window tap tapping. That's the life, free and easy love and nests. I make a wish he'll drop one feather for the use in a manspell.

I've left him tinsel for his nest so fair is fair he'll leave one feather for me.

ϕ

I have inventoried my dreams of the Old Country. My mother's broken leg appears in a narrative of a dream of war. I cannot think of the name Kulkarni without at once recalling the journey of a sea turtle through waters warm and cold, amongst the double teeth of sharks and the nimble hands of native divers. I remember from a dream a ball of wool rolling along the dirt floor of a house. The house is beside a station, which I believe is the station where my grandfather once worked as a signalman. I have had dreams of crooked rooms within a crooked house and I feel this to be the house where I was born and I know within the dream that its door is crossed with blood to safeguard me from the bright figure, brighter than sunlight, who tests the handle of the door. I know that the sound of men running and the appearance of an indecipherable script on a wall, the memory of a moon falling onto a hockey field and a library with empty shelves, which I learned later in my dream was actually a labyrinth imprisoning a monster, are all instances of my return in dreams to the Old Country. I know this because all my dreams of the Old Country are in black and white and in each dream I see a bird native to the Old Country.

I learnt long ago that native plants and animals have for many centuries been transported and smuggled between the continents of the world, and have been cultivated or have overrun native flora and fauna, but I maintain this dispersal has failed to enter my dreams, for in dreams I have never seen the colours of the vernal sparrow. Its plumage, its hooked beak, remain in my dreams in black and white.

The vernal sparrow derives its name from a legend that persists in the Old Country. The bird is said to mate only once a year on the day of the vernal equinox. It is a legend discounted by ornithologists and disproved by the bird's proliferation, yet the name persists, although it is now sometimes referred to as the ariean sparrow.

Early birdwatchers who believed in the legend attributed to this sparrow a knowledge of the universe far greater than that of humans. They argued that any living being that could coincide its seduction of a mate with the meeting of the ecliptic and the celestial equator would have known long before humanity of the curvature of the earth and proved by its survival an inherent knowledge of tide and season. So, in the Old Country, the flesh of the vernal sparrow became prized as a cure for idiocy and infertile men drained their tiny bodies and drank the blood to tune their sperm towards blessed sons. It was eaten to near extinction.

In the New Country, two hundred years after its introduction, the vernal sparrow has thrived. Ornithologists have advised citizens to line their fruit-tree trunks with foil or hang the boughs with bits of broken glass, for although the sparrow has adapted to our continent it can be frightened off by its own reflection. In the town of Tucana the vernal sparrow threatened a season's crop and so the local council erected signs in the shapes of falcons to frighten the birds away. I saw a black and white photo in the *Phoenix* once which showed tin falcons with outspread wings standing on poles along the dirt alleys of a vineyard.

# Between

What kind of life is this, to arrive here, cook and cook more the next day and then to be cleaning after cooking? My father and my sister's son, between these two pariahs I flit with my life going to the dogs. My breasts are aching for a *butcha* and my hips are burning. My tongue is wanting honey from a man's forehead and for the bruising of his temple the colour of ash he will give me a home and maybe one ayah girl as I'm no more pink in the plush of my life.

So much so I put my eye on Archer but he has such dirty habits and our stars don't match. If it wasn't such a funny thing to be thinking I'd say he reminds me of everyone and no one. How like a girl he looks when he's taking off his face with cotton balls and water. How strange his face looks coming through. In eyes how like a boy and what a fright when he took off his hair. His head is like a moon, only very black like an eclipse. But such filthy things he asks me to do. Sit like this, sit like that. Walking with a book on top of my head and not one thread on my body. And who'd know after all these years the bruising never went away and has taken on the look of maps.

ϕ

Following the Nile further, past the fourth cataract and the riverine lands, I came to Khartoum. At Khartoum the Nile divides into blue and white. I read of empires named Kush and Axum here and, recalling from earlier readings that the alphabet of Meroe, a later name for Kush, remains to this day undeciphered, I considered it a sophisticated enough civilisation to have produced the architecture of the tapestry.

On a photo of a bas-relief I saw the god of Kush. He had the head of a lion and the body of a man. I imagined the dark people of Kush, their iron spears crossed at their feet, chanting in their mysterious dialect to the Lion God, and it occurred to me as I pondered the material of his headdress that his posture and the position of his face reminded me of my grandfather's face within the cameo on his dream gravestone.

I doubted I would find my lovers at the division of the Nile. The architects of Kush seemed inclined to carve their histories on their walls. I discovered few embellishments amongst the carvings and the obelisks, but frequent in the stone were narratives of war, and simple stelae recorded the birth of sons to the pharaoh Taharqa. The walls, the monuments of Kush, I decided, were far too functional to be the smooth walls of the tapestry palace.

I pondered the Meriotic script further. Some letters of the enigmatic alphabet resembled the modern numerals for four and nine, whilst other letters were shaped like treble clefs and quavers. In the glyphs of Axum I could see sickles and half-moons, ladders and a letter in the shape of a griffin.

I recalled the etymology of the words 'God' and 'man'. From the early Sumerians to the late dynasties of Babylon, the characters for God and man simplified. 'God' was first depicted in a shape that resembled the spokes of a wheel but by the time of Babylon his character had been reduced to a shape resembling a 'T'. 'Man' began in a shape resembling a cocooned caterpillar, evolved in cuneiform through the shape of houses, then arrows, and ended as a shape I cannot find words to describe.

# No Hadja Roy

The deli man has two grown-up daughters and no wife. Nine months ago I told him it was my birthday and he gave me a Jupiter Bar. Today is my birthday and I shall tell him again.

He's no Hadja Roy, like out of glue he's made and looking sticky, but he's turned his hands to pickle and has the knack. The Lord, the Virgin knows I could eat a jar of mango pickle then be succouring up the juice.

ϕ

*I cannot remember   I cannot remember the coming of this pain into my shoulders or the disappearance of my hands   I hold a bottle between my forearms and drink   I have come here via three Harappas and have found only glimpses of memory Something in the wave of wine reminds me of flesh and mouths that sought each other in the dark   I remember the red light in the porcelain body of a man   I remember a statue on fire   I drink and I try to remember but find only the persistence of flesh, light, tongues and fire*

δ

*I have nothing upon me to prove my existence to myself   I have no wallet enclosing photos of the ones I loved or cards or documents to verify I was once a member of any club or institution Even my fingerprints are gone*

*I remember that I set out for a destination where I hoped to find an unlikely woman, moving towards some rumour in cloud or conspiracy of light whose shape verified the existence of worlds beyond the one in which I lived and yet remaining within the world in which I lived   Perhaps this other world was always amongst us, in the jungles revealed in fable, the vistas that opened in myth   I recall other men who kept photographs of women on their desks or in their wallets and I wondered if they too sought those women in hills or valleys, seas or skies foreign to their own imaginings, or if those men who turned each month to a portrait of a new woman on the calendars of their office or garage walls planned, by the seduction of days, journeys into landscapes where those women posed; desert springs where a girl in a bikini lay spread-eagled before a cactus, or the coast of Tyre where a naked swimmer emerged from the waves*

*As I approached what I expected to be the town of Caelum I saw a sign that read 'Harappa 32'   I looked again at my map but could find neither the name nor the coordinates of Harappa and pondering my journey thus far could not remember any detour or divergent road I may have taken   I wondered if the rain I drove through had washed Caelum away or if some prankster had put up a misleading sign   My map seemed useless   I felt part of a story where the narrator was dead   I drove on still expecting Caelum*

*It was on this road I first heard your voice Ganesh   You seemed within and without my mind   At first I mistook your voice for the rain and I had heard of world travellers who claimed the road could speak, that the road could keep the company of the lonely rambler   I have at times awoken with a disappointment at a dream's end or sat up straight in bed because of nightmarish beasts or dreams of falling, but your voice woke me from my flesh, as if pulse and breath were nothing but the sustenance of dreaming*

δ

*λ Manu, did you not last night wake from a dream of a bejewelled net, sinking below the riverface under the weight of rubies and diamonds, emeralds and gold, sinking far beyond the capacity of your lungs? λ*

*I entered a clay house without doors in the middle of a field I remembered fingers sorting lentils at a table long ago I wished for scars upon my body that would witch memory, some tear of skin or incision of flesh that would draw from me thoughts like ichor*

*In a bowl on the table there were grapes On the pantry shelf there was flour One ray of sunlight left a patch upon the floor Light refracted through the broken windows into octagonals of blue, of yellow, of orange and green I moved and stood in the light My shadow had hands My shadowhands took a net of light, a net of jewelled colours and cast it upon the wall Lord of Hosts, was that the dream from which you woke me?*

δ

*λ I am north and south, east and west but I cannot answer any of your questions Tonight we will drink soma and it will bring memory to your lips and you will entertain me with some talk of three Harappas I will even be your scribe as you are without hands*

*To the north of your current position is desert and you travelled east to the conjunction of waters, shedding those miles like you have shed memory The map you followed is common, available at any gas station or supermarket, and furthered in details by maps within the towns you passed through and maps within halls of the towns you passed through*

*You feel pursued but your pursuer is generations behind He will find a guide in Tucana and father a child amongst the brown streets and ochre people of Caelum   He will come to doubt the value of his search when he finds no corroboration in such details as the location of mountains and the shape of the leaves of the native trees of Kepler Park, and come to doubt the story of your travels   Then one day on a crowded main street of a town where you claimed to have lived for a time he will feel he is within a breath of you and then stop and realise, when I whisper into his ear, that he is lost and you are gone   λ*

δ

*λ Look upon the map and place yourself   Find the towns of Morning and Caelum   Then follow the map backwards to find the place of your departure   λ*

*I see a city and recall suburbs of the city whose names could be interpreted as the Valley of Spring, the Hill of the Bride   Further, I remember a city I never visited, yet from which I received letters written in a language that long ago died on my tongue   The letters were written by a woman whose own hands I imagined were written upon with henna*

*When the woman with hands written upon with henna left the Old Country with her mistress she was twenty-four years old   I imagined that the city she wrote from was named after its founder Johannes   I imagined that one day, when the uncivilised plains had been teeming with springbok and children on dusty farms were kept always within arm's distance for fear of maneaters, a young Johannes had stood bare-chested on a plateau and dreamt of the streets and stores, the libraries and town hall he would design and help build with his red, callused hands*

*I imagined that Johannes gathered in his dream city blacksmiths and tailors, millers and grocers, and after much industry and the death of numerous builders a city was raised    Generations later, when the springbok were scarce and treasured, a young woman looking up from the letter she was writing in the shade of a plateau saw the statue of a bare-chested man and she dreamed of loving him*


δ


*One night during Natraja-Puja I took my daughter Amba to the nightstalls to buy cinnamon and turmeric, rice and modaks for offerings    A yogi put a garland of lotus flowers around Amba's neck and a blind vendor gave her gold chocolate coins    The road was lit by streetlights swinging on loose wires and by gas lanterns at or near the vendors' stalls    People were hawking potato chops dipped in chilli, snakeheads preserved in aspic    Men and women called to passers-by to come and taste a licorice homebrew or rub between their fingers quality linen for shirts or shrouds    I saw my friend Jolly and his wife and daughter buying bananas and the tailor's stall was crowded with white women haggling over the price of cotton    The tailor was offering free bindi with every sale*

*I met a woman's eyes as she measured paprika into a funnel of newspaper    She slowly blinked at me    Her eyelids were painted with gold glitter and her eyelashes were long   Her hands were written upon with henna   She waved a child over to keep the till   She walked into one of the alleys of the spice markets   I followed her, past the incense vendor, down a dirt corridor and past the young boy selling tapes of the latest movie songs   The canvas roof of the markets flapped up and down and the alleys within were crowded with hawkers and customers half-hidden by smoke   A woman tried to pull me over to her blanketed stall where she sold ivory under the name of porcelain and offered a trade for Amba's hair   A man pulled back a curtain as I passed and revealed six veiled women   I kept my eyes ahead on the woman with the henna hands   I followed her outside and Amba followed me*

*What I remember next is perhaps the memory of a dream, for I am sure that Vishveshwara Lawn and its mossy, cracked fountain surrounded by a hundred lingum, its shallow bath and stone altar is located miles north of the spice markets and I remember the sound of a running river, yet no river flanked the nightstalls   I saw the woman's sari unravelled around the trunks of trees, a route of gold-laced silk that coiled the stone fountain and meandered a path across the lawn   I followed the silk passage to its end   The woman was naked in a bath, green water up to her thighs   The hem of her sari hung over the lip of the bath   Amba pulled at my shirt   I looked at the woman and then I looked at Amba and we returned, avoiding the silk route, to the trading streets   If it was a dream then I cannot explain how within a week I found the woman written upon with henna cleaning the toilets at the Tic-Toc club*

## δ

*λ Sip and remember   You walked one morning on the day of a feast to the ghats of a river λ*

*I cannot remember the name of the river but I remember boys who looked like harlequins, streaked with purple and blue dye   I remember being pelted   I remember my boat trailing colour on the water*

*Some afternoons, when I felt the first chill of an approaching storm and saw mothers come to the ghats for their children, I looked downstream to the pendulous fishing boats moored hours earlier   On the ghats yogis in saffron dhotis curved their backs full circle, folded arms and legs in figure eights   Merchants screamed of closing sales on cloves and garam though their prices rarely varied from morning to dusk   When the shadows of the boatmasts quivered on the sandstone walls and the wind cut circles into the riverface, I would sit still and breathe deeply and imagine I was preparing for a long, lone journey   I peered into the ripples around my boat for the reflection of the early moon and in my mind I crossed to the seas on the moon's surface*

*I crossed by chanting to myself the names of the seas of the moon: Mare Imbrium, Mare Crisium   I imagined the elegant seas not as craters but filled with fresh water, untroubled by tides or winds, and upon such still seas I imagined I could never age*

*I was on the road to Morning and the rain washed the road away   I came face to face with water   I calmed myself with the list of the seas of the moon and I crossed*

## δ

*I crossed into the town of Harappa and saw another man falling from the sky onto the street    I walked and walked but the main street seemed endless    The people all seemed to have a layer of skin removed    The town lay between two bridges    One of the bridges had a keystone of marble    The other bridge was wooden and the width of a child*

*A church had its window smashed    It looked as though it had been smashed from the inside    In the church grounds were shards of glass, purple and orange, green and blue*

*In a shopfront window two girls were dancing fire while a ventriloquist's dummy sang*

*I walked into a pub decorated with black and white photos    Each photo showed one corner of the intersection of the town's main streets where the pub now stands    The earliest photos showed wide, unpaved streets where a sole bearded man walked while consulting his fobwatch, lanterns hanging from poles, a horse feeding from a trough outside a general store    I moved my eyes along the line of photos and saw the store replaced by a blacksmith, then a tobacconist and furrier, then a succession of pubs all named after the body parts of a queen    The streets narrowed and were tarred    People stood beside or drove by in cars    The last photo showed the pub as it stands with its stucco walls and its bronze door plaque inscribed with the date of its opening    The bearded man appeared again in the final photo, still lost for time*

*The barmaid was wearing black lipstick and a blouse that covered her breasts but revealed her midriff    On her midriff was a tattoo of two doves poised for a kiss    I asked if there were rooms available and she nodded   She led me upstairs   She asked no payment   The room was lit by a naked red bulb   The bulb provided enough light for me to rest by and though I cannot sleep with a bright light I can neither sleep in a pitch-black room   Nor can I sleep if any doors in the room, wardrobe doors, cabinet doors, cupboard or desk drawers, are open or ajar*

*A man was asleep on the top bunk in my room   His skin looked purple, as if bruised   The room smelled of stale hookah smoke   Brown water stood in a glass   A calendar open to December hung from the wall, the days overwritten many times in adjustment to the roll of years   I looked out of a window where moonlight lit the muzzles of three dogs in the alley below   A neon sign read 'cin . . . a'   The dogs ran out of the alley*

δ

*I remember Jolly Fisher   He was a small man who looked to be moulded out of chocolate   He had a maze tattooed on his back   I have forgotten his true name but Jolly fitted him and even his wife called him Jolly   He met up with some militants engaged in the battle   Unyoking the ox, he called it   Overnight his face aged and where before he was satisfied with his pipe while he hawked the latest titles at his book corner and sorted and re-sorted the books on top of the piles, he soon was talking of the tide of history and pointing his pipebarrel at white customers, telling them to fight their own wars, to free us of their empire   Whoever was whispering into his ear persuaded him to Synder Street with a box of matches and a tin of kerosene*

*His wife brought their daughter to spit on his ashen body, still nervous with fire*

*The empire brought the Tic-Toc club and the club gave me work and a lover   So the empire was the club and the club was nothing but clipped grass and uneven tiles for the ladies to trip barefoot tipsy on   When the kitchen closed I'd upturn the card tables and remove the queens and aces stuck with chitlins to the under-rims   In the morning I'd find swords and rings, cufflinks and cigars left at the foot of the stairs   My quart of English blood employed me but I was still a breed apart   Men have no gift for being alone, I guessed the wives thought, they scatter seed on foreign soil and something native grows   I cleaned the pool for them to bathe and curse the heat, brought them iced tea and calamine lotion for the burning of their pink, pink bodies   Two children drowned during the rummy   Two coolies died from drinking the chlorine   I cleaned the billiard tables of port stains and helped carry men and women collapsed on the vapours of wine to sitting rooms   I stole pouches of tobacco for myself and dictionaries for Jolly and I'd tell him to make his money and feed his family and wait and watch the remains of empire wither*

*I cared nothing for empires after she came   I watched her dusting chairs, delivering notes with her head bowed from husband to wife, from wife to lover   I watched the men watching her and heard the women complain about the clatter of her bracelets, her sari that revealed a bellybutton encircled with glitter   She scrubbed the toilets with lime and sugar soap, drowned thick lizards in an old coffee tin filled with water, holding them under until their eyes glazed, until they exploded shit   Sometimes she gave them names, Major this and Colonel that, and blew them kisses and then submerged them    Her hands were fairer than her arms and written upon always with henna*

*I had one suit, my wedding suit, which I wore each night to work    She wore the jacket after we made love    I'd wear nothing but her belt of tin coins around my neck    Pubic hair stuck with honey to her mouth, to the lapel    We embraced in closets filled with dust and moths, kissed when the cook put his head into the oven    She covered her mouth when she smiled, said I had been bitten by many snakes*

δ

*λ Manu, fill your glass and taste    Does there linger on your tongue the aftertaste of rosemary? Do you remember the night your beloved Amba turned sixteen?    While you oiled down your arms and rubbed tiger balm on your elbows, Ida rolled balls of fried mutton mince in her palms and then handed them to Amba who shaped mashed potato around the mince and then rolled the balls in breadcrumbs    Dorothy then fried them*

*You were surprised by your daughters, by their long fingers and their cheeks touched with rouge    Soon you knew your baby Amba would meet the eyes of the men who stared at her*

*You sat and drank some country liquor and as you drank and later as you ate you started to fear for your daughters    You saw the eyes of strangers assessing their bodies and saw the hands of strangers    You feared the search for their husbands and those arrangements and the debt you'd owe the groom    You hoped they would marry a colonial    You resolved to keep them from the sun     But what white man would marry a girl too shy to show her face, who spoke a mulatto tongue?*

*You waited for them to sleep     You pulled the rosemary from the doorframe     You took down my altar*

*From tomorrow, you decided, we would speak only English in this house     We would not set out bowls of chandi or waste our meagre spice on gods     Our daughters would meet and wed the sons of the men we served and raise our grandsons in their faith of bread and wine*

*You took my murti and kindled a flame with matches and with the brittle rosemary     The clay barely smouldered so you cracked it with an axe  λ*

*No divinity needs a bribe in death as in life     I felt I knew enough of gods to know they did not need loose change     They sat at our tables, were fed before our children*

δ

*I came to my next Harappa, a city of ruins     I felt then I would find sharper directions in palm lines than in maps     I could not account for another Harappa, having left Harappa behind*

*λ  I have walked in cities yet to be built and cities soon to be destroyed     One casts its shadow over the other     The earth retains the ghosts of cities gone and the earth is overwritten many times, the lines redrawn as wars are won and lost or the citizens return to their origins     Nothing is beyond the earth, names can be exhumed     The citizens call it Harappa, why not? How could it have welcomed one further by another name?  λ*

*Queues of people lined the cobbled streets   But the monuments, the buildings had collapsed   Boys threw stones at the shards of windows   The facades of banks, museums hovered over empty lots   Faceless statues stood below marble arches, their memorial stones painted over   Carcasses of roadkill rotted in the street   Powerlines unstrung from poles touched the ground   The queues stood still and the people were silent   No one answered me when I asked what they had queued for, when I asked if they were waiting for eternity   I could find no place to sleep   I saw two men kicking and punching at each other beside an upturned table   On the ground around them chess pieces spun and rolled*

*I saw what seemed like a hundred tables on which stood many empty birdcages beneath a tarpaulin supported by eight iron poles   I presumed it a bird market so long ago abandoned that neither bird nor feather remained*

*I saw a prison attended by two guards without weapons   The walls of the prison were filled with holes   Mattresses were strung over the barbed wire and neither the prison towers were manned nor the steel gates locked   Eight black men in fatigues wandered around unmanacled within the decrepit walls*

*I wondered how I came to be amongst ruins, away from my adopted city and my home, and I wondered what bearing my name had on the beginning and continuing of my journey and the beginning and continuing of my life, but memory seemed an oasis*

δ

*λ Your parents met on a day of my festival, on the day I dice with the world   The sea was full of bathers, men wrapped in dhotis, women in saris at the shoreline holding their hems from the rush of water   Your mother's sari was threaded with silver   Your father met her eyes   Her face was veiled   She did not look away   Behind her the lights of the anchored trade ships and faces buoyed in blue water, around her the sound of prayers, the smell of green bananas   One red light pulsed on the horizon   Bare-shouldered men carried the raft that bore my garlands, my effigy*

*On their second meeting he met her eyes again   He handed her a silk-handled knife, again her face was veiled   He recognised her   He took my charms as part of his dowry   λ*

*My father once said that if he had married another woman he would have dreamed of my mother for the rest of his life*

φ

As I closed the book on the Nile I recalled one of my recurring dreams after my grandfather's death. I had moved from tombstone to tombstone, refilling jars with fresh water and cleaning the headstones of birdshit and other debris, when I saw my mother enter through the gates of the graveyard. Suddenly the light within the dream faded, as if she had brought dusk with her, as if she walked ahead of armies whose banner was night.

I dreamt once of riding a white horse into battle against armies whose flagpole fluttered with banners of night. The poles of the armies were connected to the evening sky and so their attacks came always shrouded in darkness. The soldiers of these armies had nocturnal vision and were invincible after dusk. Though our archers drew flaming arrows for the hearts of the dark warriors, though our phalanx catapulted rocks wrapped in burning rags at the feet of their horses, though we carried torches and prayed to our gods for dawn, we were slaughtered by sound and shadow.

The dream of dark armies was influenced, I am sure, by one of my aunt's stories. One summer evening in the Old Country my mother was caught in a Black Mara storm.

Every child of my mother's native city knew that a Black Mara began with a wind that created tiny pillars of whirling dust upon the street. Every child knew this sign required the covering of eyes and breathing through the nose, the seeking of shelter and the shutting of all doors. The lightning that rides the Mara seems horizontal and silent. The sky seems to crack within the jagged borders of horizon and light. Then night seems to fall upon the earth. Black Maras came and passed within four minutes, yet could blind a child. The storms, legend told, were vicious enough to gift the blinded with a glimpse of their future loves, the loves they would never see.

My mother was tending her herbpots when the wind crept between her legs. The stalks of basil and coriander were tender. My mother knew the storm would rip them from the dirt. She sought a board or bag to shield them. She found some paper bags. The wind shredded them in her hands.

The pillars of dust around her soon seemed solid enough to lean upon. She pushed through into the house but the wind held the door against closure. Lightning moved across the sky like a graph of the wind. My mother placed a handkerchief over her mouth and found swimming goggles to cover her eyes. The lightning stopped but the wind and dust fell thick within the house and my mother crouched beneath a table and saw the falling of the midday dusk. The wind then made a dull, prolonged sound that became silence. The black storm passed.

My mother began to clean up in the aftermath, avoiding the use of water. Even tears could slush the house, she knew. She swept. She pulled the plastic coverings from the sofa, threw out the gritty bread. My grandparents returned from the markets to a clean house and a daughter in a disguise of earth. Clean flesh encircled her eyes. My mother asked my grandparents about the face she had glimpsed in the storm. She wondered if the man with oily hair and mascaraed eyes was her future beau. She wondered how she could have seen and yet retain her sight. My grandparents assured her she had seen the face of her sister's love and that night made arrangements for my mother to transfer to the school of the sisters of Vaudois.

## Monkey

I have to tell you now, no monkey see, monkey do. Your papa was a little touched and thought that one day he would fly. Some old idiot in some old book said these things and so he came to think that if only he kept his mouth shut and ate barely nothing or nothing at all he would fly, but like I said to him that means any old lonely beggar will one day go off like a hawk. I'm only telling you in case you've got some big ideas.

ϕ

I am reminded of Mirren when in the hours approaching dusk I see the swaying branches of the jacarandas and palm trees, the eucalypts and kaly oaks in the grounds of the Town Hall.

The kaly oak is the common name of the *Casuarina Kalymna*, a tree native to the New Country. Its bark is black and it populates the banks of creeks and billabongs. Its seed requires a burst of heat to germinate and thus it survives bushfires. The botanist L'Heritier once described the leaves as being in the shape of scimitars and kept a leaf of the kaly oak framed beside his bed. The poet of the City of Kind Hearts, Henry David Thoreau, records somewhere in his journals a fascination for the kaly and for the function of its bark.

Some nights I used to watch the branches of the kaly oak while Mirren showered. I'd hear the water falling and I'd hear her singing and I'd hear the echo of her singing and see the swaying shadows of the leaves. When she emerged from the shower with one towel wrapped around her body and one wrapped around her head I'd see the freckles on her thighs and her shoulders. Steam would rise from her body. Her skin seemed paler after she showered.

So perhaps it was misleading for me to write that I thought of Mirren whenever I heard or said, or read or wrote the word 'love', for on many occasions, even on the mid-morning of last Adamsday when I stared at the eyes of the god's lover, or when I imagined the swaying trees, an image of Mirren came into my mind—Mirren dancing, Mirren's two-fingered wave—and I felt crestfallen. I felt an uneasiness like the lingering afterthoughts of nightmares, the dread that persisted in waking hours. Indeed, in books I have read or songs I have heard, a jilted suitor or betrayed wife will bemoan the loss of their lover and wonder if their long walks and long dinners, the exchange of secrets and the meeting of bodies were all experiences remembered from a dream. The writer or singer even sometimes wonders whether the places they met, the bedrooms and the city squares, the gardens and the restaurants, only existed in dreams of their lover, and on returning to the sites of courtship or consummation, whether physically or in their mind, they find the private table gone and the restaurant closed, the hidden circle of lawn dug up and the garden in ruin.

One evening before dusk Mirren and I searched in the grounds of the Town Hall for the nest of fledgling bloodbirds that awoke us every morning and disturbed us every evening. We walked amongst the jacarandas and oaks, the eucalypts and palm trees, stopping beneath each tree and looking up into the maze of branches. When the wind blew Mirren put her hands up to shield her eyes from a shaft or network of sunlight and when the wind stopped she peered deep into the leaves and tilted her head to one side, hoping the call of a bloodbird would betray the nest.

I wandered off toward the perimeter of the grounds where a jacaranda stood, its branches hanging low to the ground, its flowers seemingly woven together. I walked in under the canopy of branches. I could see nothing outside the curtain made by the branches and the only light came in spots and speckles. I thought I heard someone call my name. I pushed my head through the hanging branches.

I saw Mirren standing beneath a kaly oak, one hand gesturing me forward, the other pointing up into the tree. Her mouth was moving but I could only hear the sounds of traffic and wind. As I walked toward her I realised that she was mouthing words without sound. The shadows of the branches moved across her face as her mouth moved. She seemed to be talking shadow. She half-closed her mouth as I neared her and mimed the flapping of wings and pointed to the tree, and the shadows continued in ill-defined circles across her face as if reliant upon the circularity of her breath, shading then revealing her eyes. She looked at me, perhaps expecting some mimed gesture in reply. Then, as I was within arm's length of her, the wind changed and the sun scrolled upon Mirren's face a pattern of shadow that seemed like the writings of an ancient language, the glyphs of a civilisation long dead. I imagined myself searching the world for speakers of the dead language, examining the exhumed tablets of buried cities, attempting to decode the words upon Mirren's face, words of a recipe or spell that would tame or sate desire.

I followed the line of Mirren's finger into the tree. After my eyes had focused on the details of leaf and branch I saw a tattered nest made of twigs and drinking straws, lined with tinsel and spotted with holes the size of thumbnails. Together we poked at the ground beneath our feet for broken eggs or the hairless chicks of bloodbirds.

The lights of the second floor of the Town Hall came on and I could see the profile of a man in one of the porthole windows. The Town Hall had been designed to resemble the ship our city was named after, with mast-like flagpoles and a bust of Nike in the hall's foyer. The mayor's chambers stood at the top of curved wooden staircases, in the place where I presumed the architect had imagined the captain's quarters. Indeed, on nights at the Bar Panther I had overheard the civil servants refer to their offices as the galleys.

When the man in the window put on his feathered hat and tasselled gown I recognised the profile of the mayor.

I have never met the mayor. I'd seen him in his ceremonial robes and hat at the library opening and other civic events but we had never shaken hands or exchanged greetings. I had received my commission to find the blue god after responding to an advertisement on the library noticeboard. The ad offered award rates to any historian or researcher who could find the origins and artist of the tapestry. The ad read that the tapestry would be taken down and replaced with a seascape by a local artist if it possessed no historical worth, though the ad also stressed that the figures of the tapestry would be remembered in future Adamsday parades. The job offered basic pay until the search concluded or up to a maximum of twelve months and stated that all applicants should write to the head librarian, beside whose name was the insignia of our quarter—the brass spire of St Ambrose's Church overlooking an anchor three stylised waves deep.

I was either the sole applicant or my propinquity to the library persuaded the city to favour me. I began my search immediately, writing to textile galleries, consulting books on the loom, but then realised that my search could end within a month. I took time off and used one monthly cheque to fund a daytrip to the Rheita Valley and ventured inland one weekend to the source of Hevel River where my grandfather and I had once fished. I drank red wine from bottles sheathed in brown paper on the train to Blue Lake station and caught a bus to my hotel where I drank more wine until I fell asleep on my starched bed hungry and drunk. I awoke the next morning and walked along a signposted road to the river. I remembered the spot where my grandfather had once stood kneedeep in water, a spangled fly on his line, but I remembered the banks as secluded and untamed, a bend of river frequented by knowing fishermen who would whisper its coordinates only in the company of their sons, yet before me that day I saw barbecues and toilets, rubbish bins and an oarboat tied to a tree.

The day I fished with my grandfather I caught nothing and grew bored. I had my favourite toy with me, a balsawood plane which my grandfather had ordered from the Old Country for my eighth birthday. The plane had my name stencilled on its wings and its pilot was a man made out of wired beads.

I cannot now nor could I then account for what I did. I threw my plane out onto the river, knowing it would be lost. I tried to catch it back as soon as I threw it. The plane flew for a few metres, skidded out onto the water and sank under the river's weight. My grandfather turned and saw it submerge. He threw down his line and waded out further into the water. He dived down. He was underwater for a long time. He re-emerged with a fish in his hand but without the plane.

Over our dinner of fried trout and boiled potatoes he told me to forget the plane and said that for my next birthday he would take the money he had saved and flush it down the toilet. However, on the way home he stopped at a souvenir shop in Caelum and bought me a new toy.

The toy was a plastic figure of the bushranger Macquarie in his legendary pose, a pistol in his left hand pointing out, the gun in his right hand placed against his own temple. Legend said that Macquarie's stance threatened to halve the trackers' reward and their confusion allowed him time to mount his fabled horse Bucephalus and leap over Blue Lake. When we arrived home my aunt was unhappy with the woollen scarf my grandfather had bought her and begged the bushranger from me for her glass world.

# Jackwitch

Say you make a paste with basil and fishscale. Then you wipe it on Jack's doorstep and say Jack, Jack, Jack, Jack. Then when the moon turns you light one red candle and that night and the next day you close your mouth to food and water. Then you leave a chair within a circle. Who's to say you'll not soon have a good spread of chutneys and pickles?

ϕ

I am sitting and writing on the balcony of my home, a terrace house which was once used as an op-shop for the Society of St Therese. When Mirren first moved in here she cleaned out the bottom floor, packing the chipped plates and bric-à-brac in boxes for the council workers to collect on collection day. She took what she needed upstairs: wine bottles to use as candleholders, glasses, cutlery, fake jewellery. She saved the detective novels but packed the romances she would never read and textbooks on maths and physics into milk crates, which she stored with the stock the Society had asked her to save, but which they never came to reclaim.

When I moved in with her the bottom floor was unfurnished, the basement full of junk. I moved my few belongings—my clarinet and a suitcase of clothes, my music books and two tape recorders—into the room beside hers. The shopfront window was hung with uneven curtains. Any passer-by could peer in at the corners of the window and see the open, empty till on the oak counter, the bare walls marked by light rectangles from where pictures had once hung. The carpet retained the impressions left by a decade of heavy wardrobes, the feet of chairs.

Mirren was thirty-five years old when we first met. She had one green eye and one brown eye and she often tied her curly red hair back with a bandanna. She had once assumed the name of her dead sister Maya as a stage name when she worked as a magician's assistant in the clubs and pubs, at the office and children's parties in her former city. She suffered from hayfever which she treated with crystals and water diets and twice a year she visited a tarot-card reader. She had a half-sister named Lara whom she had last seen in the City of Saints six years before. Lara had been trying to find Mirren. In the month before Mirren left she showed me a black and white photo of herself in the public notices of the *Phoenix* newspaper. She had short black hair in the three-year-old photograph and her face seemed rounder. At first I saw no resemblance between the woman in the photograph and the woman who sat beside me, but when I concentrated on the eyes, their deep setting and their disparity in shade from left to right, I saw Mirren.

What I had thought of as my first meeting with Mirren was in fact our second meeting. A year after her disappearance I recalled that she had been part of a procession of saffron robes and tambourines in the city square. I had gone that day to watch a movie with my aunt and we stopped with many other pedestrians to watch the dancing men and women, boys and girls. A woman with short black hair, her body wrapped in a sari but her midriff bare, her eyelashes sprinkled with glitter, handed out leaflets to the audience, inviting all to a feast.

One day last year, on one of my daily walks, I saw a girl placing leaflets beneath the windscreen wipers of cars and I remembered Mirren.

On the occasion which I believed for a long time to be our first meeting, Mirren passed me as I was leaving the library. I left the library and followed her as she walked down the street. For a minute we were separated by pedestrians but I could see her red curly hair bouncing up ahead. She entered a café. I followed her in, though the café had a 'Closed' sign on the door.

Mirren was sitting at a table, alone in the café, holding a small pocket mirror up to her face.

When I was a child, in the years before I attended kindergarten, my Aunt Ida would take me shopping with her. On shopping days my aunt would wake earlier than her usual six o'clock and prepare my grandfather's breakfast and lunch. Then, after my grandfather had left for work, she would wake me and undress me and lead me to the shower. My aunt would wrap a cake of soap—I always remember it as lavender soap—in a facecloth, and as the water washed over my body she would scrub first my shoulders and chest, then my underarms and between my legs. Once or twice she pulled on my foreskin and said that it would soon have to come off. She then turned the shower off and repeated the scrubbing, this time including my face and behind my ears. Then she shampooed my hair and rubbed a teaspoon of rosemary oil into my scalp. I would close my eyes. She would count to twenty. I would then feel the water running through my hair and feel my body shed the soap and when I reopened my eyes I would see my aunt's hair flecked with water and her hands wringing the facecloth. Sometimes she would wonder aloud how a boy could become so filthy playing inside all day. At other times, after she had shampooed my hair, she would mould it into the shape of a horn and tell me that I was the last of the unicorns.

While I dried my body my aunt would dry my hair. My aunt would then powder my face and choose an outfit for me to wear. Sometimes she made me wear a pink skirt with a blue top and at other times she made me wear a blue top with puffy sleeves and a denim skirt with an embroidered red heart on the thigh. She dressed me in sandals and pastel-coloured runners.

After my aunt had dressed me she would open the cupboard where she kept her wigs. The cupboard smelt of rosemary. Grey and grey-streaked black horsehair wigs rested on foam heads. The pores of foam when viewed close up reminded me of the surface of the moon, and I remember nights when the cupboard door was open and the heads seemed like six small moons in alignment and I imagined the alignment foretold the coming of my father.

My aunt combed my hair back and stuck a pin into my fringe. She took a short dark wig from one of the foam heads and placed it on my head. Often the wig was loose and if I moved my head from left to right and made the wig uneven my aunt would slap me on the back of the head or on the back. Sometimes she slapped my face and then would have to reapply the powder.

Once Aunt Ida had straightened and secured the wig, she dabbed my cheeks with rouge. She would curse my dark skin beneath her breath. She then painted my lips with henna, outlining them with a red lip pencil. She used tweezers to pull out my eyebrows, refining them to clean pointed arcs. My eyes watered or I cried. Sometimes I wore a bow, sometimes a hat. She held a mirror up for me to see myself.

I walked with my aunt down the supermarket aisles. She pushed the shopping trolley. She called me Sarita. She asked me to fetch her things from shelves I could barely reach. As I stretched the hem of my skirt would hitch up, revealing a glimpse of underwear. My aunt would giggle, her hand covering her mouth. I cannot remember if people stared at me. I remember though that my aunt seemed to prefer me as a girl. I heard other women compliment my aunt on my eyebrows or the redness of my cheeks.

My aunt called it our private game and forbade me from telling my grandfather. She told me that Papa would hit her if he found out and when we returned home she was careful to remove all traces of lipstick and rouge and she dabbed behind my ears with methylated spirits to conceal the smell of perfume. The spirits stung.

In repayment for my silence my aunt would buy me a book of crosswords or dot-to-dot puzzles. If there was money left over my aunt would treat herself to a bag of candy bananas, which we would share on the bus home.

Often the puzzles were apparent long before I joined the dots, the shapes of dragons and crabs visibly mapped out. But the crosswords were always left unfinished, my aunt and grandfather unable to assist me with slang or famous people.

Mirren turned her compact mirror to face me as I entered the café. The glass of the mirror had cracked into the shape of a three-pronged fork. She asked me if I recognised the symbol. She spoke with an accent I had never before heard.

I shook my head.

Mirren walked into the kitchen, her long blue skirt scraping the floor and making a sound like the ruffling of feathers. I sat down across from where she had been sitting. She emerged in the doorway of the kitchen holding a notepad and wearing an apron. Her hair was drawn back from her face.

She asked me what I would like and then, before I answered, offered to make something for us both. I nodded. I looked at Mirren as she looked at me.

She walked back into the kitchen. A ringlet of her hair fell down across her left shoulder. I got up and put a song on the jukebox. The song was called 'Smithsonian Blues' by a blues singer named Blind Dog Harvey, a man who looks like he's been sculpted out of bronze. I hummed along and then I heard Mirren singing so I stopped humming and listened. Her accent disappeared when she sang.

I sat down as Mirren came back and placed two plates of fried eggs and toast on the table. She put a basket of chips between us and poured two cups of coffee. As we shared the chips our hands brushed.

## A princess for a troll

What a hullabaloo has come into my sleep thinking of this Jack Macquarie. Be it like a lesson. Who knows of the heart? Even a princess can fall for a troll if I am liking a pink man with a bald head like it's made from cream. And of course he will give me his heart, why not? I've kept my figure because luckily I don't have a tooth for sweets. And I say a prayer to Mary and one to Amba that he will be an Aries, for Aries and Capricorn make good stars together.

ϕ

Mirren held the mirror's face to me again. She said that the glass of her compact mirror had cracked into the shape of the eohl. She said that when she had first seen the fractured glass she had heard in her mind the sound of pages turning and felt an uneasiness she could not account for. But as she stared at me she had suddenly remembered the patterns on stones.

Mirren had dated a young man at university who had taught her about runestones. He had held each stone before her eyes and said their name aloud—the eohl, the haegal,—before casting them onto a cloth printed like a target whose circles represented being, thinking and doing. As the stones landed he consulted a vellum-bound book to divine their meaning. He read Mirren's cast and recommended that she seek her inner magic, for the eohl was in the circle of her being.

Mirren took a sheet of paper from a drawer behind the counter. She then took a pen from a pencilcase in her bag. She drew a circle on the paper. She said it was the circle of being. Around that she drew another circle, the circle of thinking, and finally she drew a circle around the two circles, the circle of doing.


From newspaper and radio interviews with sociologists I have learnt that generally the income of our citizens is in proportion to the distance they live from the city. Though I presume that there are numerous exceptions to this, such as the traders who work in the city and feel it uncivilised to live so near their toil, and others who simply prefer the views of mountains and the taste of keener air, most people, I have read or heard about, take their work and pay their rent in circles that radiate out from the GPO, alongside men and women of similar incomes. Of course, between these bands travel the homeless and the soaks, who squat in the disused railyards near Eddington Street or live beneath sheets of corrugated iron in the Volkoff Tunnel, but the citizens of my city, it seems, seek and find alike. Even the disinherited, those born in salt, find their neighbours in the underclass and share their fagends over barrelfires the way the suburban share their rakes.

So as I stared at what in time I came to think of as Mirren's map of life, I further daydreamed of mapping the residences of love and grief within my city. In my mind pulsing circles throbbed from the city's heart into boroughs where widowed neighbours held their private dances, or called in clairvoyants to witch some afterword over milky tea and arrowroot. As the city localised its dead, so I dreamed it housed its lovers in streets named after dead poets and hounded its living poets into the insomniac ghettos, its lonely into the staccato streetlights of the avenues of suicides.

Mirren's boyfriend had instructed her to stay still. He had instructed her that the cast of the eohl into her circle of being required that she await the coming of magic by meditating and allowing her thoughts to guide her. As Mirren spoke there came into my mind an image of her sitting in the scimitar shaped shadows of the kaly oak, her hands spread outward on her crossed legs, awaiting the words of a stone.

Mirren talked throughout the meal and when it was finished she lit a small cheroot cigar. She blew smoke rings. She took some change out of her purse and left it on the table. Then she took off the apron and wrote something on the notepad and left it on the counter. I asked her why she was paying and she said she didn't work in the café. She said she had simply entered, found no one to serve her and decided to make us both a meal. Then she said it was time we went.

I left Mirren that day and walked to my grandfather's house. I wondered what city Mirren had come from originally and wondered how a foreigner to my city might navigate its streets.

I knew well the streets of my city and their narration, the flagstone boulevards that led to the coastal piers, the turn-off to the Russell Highway that led to the Altai Mountains, the Botanical Gardens and its winding walks, the short cuts through car parks. As I walked my familiar route home—past St Ambrose's, left onto Kerr Street and then against the run of numbers along Wheeler, from 112 to 48—I imagined Mirren's disorientation, the comfort of monuments and the trail of numbers like breadcrumbs to whatever destination she toured to, to whatever destination she called home.

In my search I came upon the great and ancient city of Teotihuacan and I saw within its topography avenues of death and pyramids of the moon. Into walls were cut circles for the gods of the sun to appear. Archaeologists had uncovered burial sites of kings and pecked crosses that seemed to be city grids, but nowhere in the ruins did they find monuments to love or lovers. I discounted those ancient citizens, though the canals seemed an ideal place for the meeting of lovers and they lived by forests which could shield lovers from jealous eyes. I doubted they believed in a god of love. The circles through which the vernal gods projected sunlight onto temple walls were discovered long after the lovers I imagined had walked the avenues of death.

The buildings and monuments scored upon the earth to save a tribe and ensure the propagation of the tribe stayed the wind and weather of a thousand years, while the bones of the tribe powdered in the ground. Pyramids survived invasion and decay whereas lovers, killed by disease or exiled by the failure of crops, were unmarked by the city and the earth.

On many occasions I took Mirren on sightseeing trips through my city, repeating to her the names of native plants or explaining to her the legends that accompanied monuments. She seemed unimpressed by the landmarks of my city and dismissed with an aversion of her eyes the flowering gardens and secluded paths and called the land itself juvenile and untamed.

A city legend told that in the year after we held the Olympic Games, a sculpture of an athlete was commissioned by the presiding mayor. The sculpture was to stand in the Botanical Gardens, within a circle of acacia, the athlete holding a javelin which would point directly at the noon sun. An artist, whose name I have forgotten, was commissioned and given one year to complete the sculpture.

At the unveiling, when the satin drape was pulled from the sculpture, the mayor and the press, the civic fathers and the gathered crowd stood in silence. The athlete had large breasts and a penis. The sculptor claimed the athlete was in the pose of a high jumper clearing the bar but the pose was interpreted as a sexual position. The mayor called for the statue to be covered, for the press to withhold their photographs. Workmen dismantled the bronze hermaphrodite and carried it away. The artist fled the city. A new work was commissioned.

The next year a javelin thrower was unveiled. It made the cover of the *Phoenix* and editorials praised it. The mayor's office received a hundred letters a day remarking on the classical pose, the accuracy of the spear at noon. The sculpture became a meeting place for tourists and truants, for friends and first dates. Within a month or so the javelin was stolen, then replaced, stolen and replaced again. Guards were deployed, then judged a waste of city funds. The guards were withdrawn. The javelin disappeared. The civic fathers deemed its replacement pointless. The athlete, without the javelin, retained his expression of exertion, his fist clenched and upraised. The citizens nicknamed him 'Tantrum'. His bronze groin, his bronze torso were defaced nightly with spraypaint and with shit.

## What a god wants

One god saw your mummy taken with the ills and yet golden in her face, her hands. And wanting what a god wants, for in the end he is a man, he said to her when she was sleeping, Come and see this garden without love gone to seed. Come and be my love and this garden will grow. Now your mummy was a practical woman with an eye out for a deal and must have said, Well, bugger this, here's one hand with a garden and a god, another hand with the small *pisa* of life, why not take the garden and end it?

So your nana, let's just say for the comfort of the table, had to stay behind in case this god turned out to be a wastrel and unfit, gallivanting or not bringing home good wages. And anyway you must be remembering a mother can no more leave her child than December leave the year.

ϕ

While searching I was reminded of trackers and hunters, beasts and humans who could read the landscape. I coveted the knowledge required to see a potential feast in a drop of blood, or to read a man's mind in his tracks. Amongst the native population legends told of men who had found lost children by following a path to the moon, who had held dry roots in their hands and correctly named the place, the hour, the escapee would fall. I have heard naturalists describe the hunting tricks of native carnivores, wings that feel the ripe wind, teeth that sense the meat of day.

Some mornings after the recalling of dreams I descend the stairs of my house and take a long walk around the streets of my city. Sometimes I walk up Synder Street and cross the paths that lead through the Botanical Gardens, pausing some mornings to read and touch the engraved names on the war memorial at Bride's Hill, or I walk further down to Penrose Street, past the shopping centre and cafés of Rees Road, which runs parallel to Schiller River, where I might look up and see the light towers of the football stadium, or hear, as if I am being pursued by music, the song of a busker coming from the steps of the city square. On occasions in the streets of my city I see the back doors of meat vans swing open and see the carcasses of pigs strung from hooks by their snouts, surrounded by a mist that makes their skin glisten. I see men outside pubs waiting for them to open, the queues outside the unemployment offices, workers having their last cigarettes before entering office buildings, children smoking in alleys. I hear the honking of horns and watch men watch the secretaries of Carter Road. I see people hanging from hooks in trams, newspaper boys scuttling between moving cars.

I am always aware that any of the faces I pass on my walks may appear later in my dreams, may become citizens of my dream city. I consider what legends, what folklore may be shared between the city of my dreams and the city of my waking hours. I wonder whether in both cities it is believed that Thursday's fine is Friday's rain, that an electrocuted bat means a baby soon.

I search for Mirren's face in the people I pass. I search for aspects of her, a similar tint of eye or grace of walk. I dream I see the tracks of Mirren, a thread of dress, the wet impression of a heel. If I owned a photo of her I would have opened my wallet to any passer-by. I would have described to any shop clerk the changing colour of her hair, outlined for a fellow commuter the tiny birthmark on her cheek. Perhaps like a native tracker I should have followed a path to the moon.

On my walks I always check the Bar Panther, the pub

where Mirren and I would drink, to see if she'd returned. The Bar Panther was a large black brick building with chrome tables and chairs, located on the street named after the war. It was my local pub, a place where I could nod over my glass to the people I often ignored in the street but whom I knew to be neighbours. The bar often had amateur nights where Archer promised to perform one day and where incompetent jugglers and comedians, singers and pianists were booed off stage. The charm of such nights, it seemed to me, was the opportunity to shout down the dreams of your neighbours. It seemed a peculiar habit of our citizens to delight in the failed ambitions of other citizens.

One night, returning from the Bar Panther, Mirren and I found our house had been broken into. We had left the till open to show any passing thief the empty coinslots, and when we returned we found the till closed and full of five-cent pieces. Nothing as far as we could remember was missing. The thief was welcome to whatever glasses and crockery, whatever used clothes or costume jewellery they wanted. Neither of us owned anything of value. Even the fridge was empty. We went downstairs to check the stock in the basement. Books had been emptied out of boxes and clothes taken out of plastic bags and off hangers. Still we found nothing missing, nothing to the value of one dollar.

That night Mirren had a dream. She rushed into my room in her nightdress and woke me up. She had fine stubble on her thighs and on her calves. Her eyes were still narrow with sleep. Her skin seemed to hang from her, as if it were a disguise of skin. She told me that in her dream we slept while the dead came to the basement to reclaim their belongings. The dead were invisible. All she saw were the arms of jackets being filled out. Bodies were fitted into long floral dresses and the pages of books were turned. Invisible hands moved chess pieces on a board without kings. Marbles rolled on the floor.

Mirren said that she remained asleep while her dreamself watched the dead. Her dreamself was angered by her sleeping body and irritated by the theft, the play of ghosts. Mirren's dreamself scolded spirits, claimed to see their invisible bodies, and when they would not leave the house the dreamself came into my room and woke me.

# Good

He was not a good man. My mother was a saint compared to him, every day the washing and the cooking and he'd be out at Agra with some woman or the idea of some woman. But I'm thinking he had the concerns of a good man. Food and roof and shoes and clothes. Yet he had no idea of the debt you owed the heart. He would have been a better father to have left me with my mother. He could have had a bird's life and saved me a skin of bruises, who knows what tables the Old Country had set waiting for me? Hadja Roy had these sweet words for a song, something about men who give flowers and hours but Daddy gave you all his time and made the flowers flower, or either Daddy he put the hours in the flowers. But whatever those words your papa was not that Daddy.

ϕ

I found I could account for his colour. In pages on the gods of Greece, on Zeus and Diana, Apollo and 'ox-eyed' Hera, I found a reference to the poet Homer. Homer used the word 'ichor' to describe the blue blood of gods. The blue blood of gods ensured their immortality. The word 'ichor' now describes a watery substance, or refers to the blood of insects, but in Homer's work and time it denoted a divine aristocracy.

Refreshed by this small find I moved back and forth between the pages of the book, each god a bridge to another, each river flowing with a residing spirit. I saw a sculpture of Tyche, the goddess of fortune, sitting on a rock with the River Orontes at her feet. The River Orontes was depicted in the sculpture as a young man, and from the vantage of the reader Tyche appeared to be surfing on the youth's back. Fortune was a spirit which attached itself to the body of a female so that her divinity was invisible, and Orontes seemed pale and youthful, far too young to mark him as my god.

The next time I met Mirren she was walking toward Hevel River. On the banks of the river an old gypsy woman reads tarot cards. The only payment the gypsy asks is a loaf of bread to feed the pigeons that flock around her. The civic fathers once asked the police to remove her because the pigeons shat on the heads of tourists, but the tourists themselves shouted at the police and followed her to the opposite bank. She is now considered a city icon. Mirren was going to consult the cards when I saw her. We walked together for a while.

Mirren told me of a dream. When she was six years old she had a nightmare about the cartoon characters Heckyl and Jeckyl, whom she repeatedly referred to as Jekyll and Hyde. In her nightmare the crows attacked a straw man in a field of corn and ripped out its button eyes and set upon its body of straw until all that remained was the drawstring from its pants and the cross it hung upon. The headsack with the seamed mouth was torn and tattered. The ragged cuffs were shredded. The crows sat in a bed of the strawman's body and ate until their stomachs stretched and then they picked their teeth with straw.

# Fingerweb

While my mother knitted, Amba and I would play this game with a ball of wool. Sometimes she'd make me be a mouse and push the ball with my nose. Sometimes we'd make a hopping game or fingerweb. When your fingers were ravelled with wool you could make shadows of butterflies and bats on the wall and to each other they would tell a story. We had all sorts of games and fun to be having and only seeing her face I could see her face was keeping one or two kinds of secrets. Such a face whose sweetness never left even when she was leaving.

ɸ

I left Mirren as we neared the river and returned home. I walked into the kitchen. Archer was sitting at the kitchen table with his hands in his lap and a beer in front of him. My aunt was standing near the stove, dipping croquettes of muttonmince in eggwash and then rolling them in breadcrumbs. In a bowl on the kitchen windowsill riceballs were soaking in purple dye.

Archer took a coin out of his pocket when he saw me. He twirled the coin over each of his fingers and then pulled another larger coin from his nose. He made both coins disappear. Behind him the dog jumped up on the kitchen window and looked in and growled. My aunt began singing a song and Archer joined in.

Archer was a small man who seemed to hop when he walked. When he lived in the Old Country he worked in a travelling menagerie as a clown and sometimes as an acrobat. He had at other times in his life been a snakecharmer and juggler. He had had short-term jobs since his arrival in my city as a post office clerk and cleaner. He arrived here after we did, but he has always seemed to be present in my life. One of my earliest memories involves Archer disembarking from an aeroplane wearing a suit whose lapels looked like wings and a foam nose the size and colour of an orange.

I remember spending many nights at Archer's flat whilst I was growing up and on many occasions I was sent to him with leftovers from our table: giblet fry and dhal, or curried tongue that would be stale within a day and was too rich to feed the dog. Archer lived in a basement flat with one window. The window faced the street but was covered in newspaper which told in faded print of the abandonment of a search for three children and a call-up of merchant seamen. The flat had only two rooms: a bathroom and a living room. Archer slept on a sofa bed with a floral design whose twisting bouquets and wreaths reminded me of my grandfather's native language. A hotplate unfolded from one of the walls and a dusty bulb hung from the ceiling and cast a butter-coloured light over the room. One wall of the living room was covered with pictures torn from magazines of men and women in acts of, or nearing, sexual intercourse. On some of the pages women stood or lay in acts of seduction while the shadows of men fell across their bodies. On other pages hands held other hands as lips pursed for a kiss. Tongues coiled and breasts hung close to tongues. One woman winked at the camera while holding a penis in her right hand. On the opposite wall hung a map of the planets in a line receding from the sun to Pluto but missing Jupiter. Above the map Archer had stapled the covers of his favourite albums: Paul Robeson at Carnegie Hall and Zamfir's *Pipes of Love*.

In one corner of the room a stack of pornographic magazines and the *Kama Sutra*, books of erotic art and stories with missing pages were covered by an oilcloth. Although Archer always covered his books and magazines when he had visitors, he never once removed the couples from his walls. He argued with my grandfather that the same poses could be seen carved into any temple wall in the Old Country. On the many occasions I had taken food to Archer I looked through his collection and examined the pages of copulating couples and peered at the genitals of women veiled in silk or lace. I felt welcomed by their eyes and postures into the pages of a world where, it seemed, I could have sex in various positions with various women without ever once being in love.

There was, however, a picture in one of Archer's books which scared me. Centuries ago, in the City of Lilies, a love affair had begun between the son and daughter of rival families, and, as punishment for the consummation of this affair and because the lovers vowed never to relinquish their love for one another, the rival families plotted together and imprisoned the lovers in a room the size of a shower cubicle and into the room they released a million moths. In the illustration for the story a partly decomposed man held his face up to be kissed by a skeletal woman in whose arms he was being held. His fingers had slid around her lower vertebrae. A pile of moths covered the bones of their feet. Although the illustration terrified me—I am still today disconcerted by the manic flight of moths and the dusting of their wings—I always sought out the book from Archer's collection, but I held the page at an angle to my face, as if afraid of seeing what I had placed before my own eyes.

A year before I met Mirren my aunt had decided that it was time for me to have a lover. She took the pigs' ribs which she boiled up weekly for the dog and stripped the bones of meat. She sprinkled the bones with salt and ginger powder and then she wrapped them in a hessian bag into which she placed a new candle and a cut red apple. She placed the hessian bag in an earthenware jar at the crossroads of the streets Wald and Newton. The next morning we found the smashed jar but the bones had gone, which my aunt interpreted as a good sign.

I prayed at the time for my aunt's witchcraft to work. Some nights I stayed awake thinking over the girls in Archer's magazines, girls with blonde hair and brown pubic hair or with pierced nipples and vulvas. I imagined fucking these women in the aisles of churches or in secluded spots in public parks. Indeed, throughout my pubescent years a secluded garden path or a circle of hidden lawn immediately tuned my mind to sex, and I memorised the places where in my mind I took the women from magazines in carnal embraces on public land: the rotunda of the Botanical Gardens, behind the border of hedges at the abandoned lighthouse.

During puberty I watched many movies filmed in the City of Falling Stars. The movies were made especially for boys of my own age, movies whose plot was driven by a young hero's quest to have sex with a woman who seemed inaccessible. The hero in movies such as *Boy Scouts* and *River Girls* connived and plotted to glimpse nude the impossible girl, and after successive failed attempts at laying his hands on her body, in episodes that usually involved wet clothing or the upstaging of a rival suitor, finally made love with her. The girl would realise, after being stalked or stripped by the hero, whose eye she had first glimpsed in the knothole of a shower, that he was in truth a resourceful young man who would always truly love her. Often their relationship would be crowned at the prom or at the end of an unlikely race, much to the chagrin of the girl's parents or the boy's parents, the principal or the dean, though the dean's wife might have looked wistfully on. I never once doubted that some or all of these things would one day happen to me.

Though I had scant knowledge of my aunt's lovecraft, I disbelieved that a year after the charmed bones were scattered at a crossroad her spell brought Mirren into my life, that wax and apple, salt and bone had witched me a potential lover. I actually considered whether she had hexed the road my grandfather took towards Morning.

## Goat

Jack Macquarie gave me a bottle of Billy Goat plum jam. Am I a goat, does he think? Anyways I can taste cinnamon in it. His last bits of hair are the colour of cinnamon. His pits, his thing will smell of cinnamon. Who is he not to fall in love with me? I am the colour of something delicious and I've kept my figure and what the hell does he think comes from using rosemary every evening on my wighair and sweet almond oil on my skin? Who has to worry, not someone who maintains her looks and doesn't go overboard on sweets, godknows no man has any idea.

φ

*Ganesh, this soma suddenly has the taste of blood*
    λ *Your grandfather hunted with guns and knives    He was English and had English friends who sometimes hunted with him    When you were a child he'd wittle animals from ginger for you and enact the stalking of tiger and the pits dug for boar    When a boar was killed they brought it home and immersed it in boiling water    The women peeled the skin with knives sharpened by the men on stones*

    *It was legend amongst hunters of boar that he once killed a male while bloody and flattened to the ground    He was returning from a luckless hunt with the rest of his party    He had killed for trophies, not for meat: a falcon, a monkey, which took four minutes to die    He had shot a stray dog because the gun felt urgent in his hand*

    *During the hunt he had been sitting in a tree when a python had coiled slowly around his waist    He waited till its grip tightened then grabbed the head and hucked it off    The muscles along the python's back had tensed    Members of his party had to climb the tree and uncoil him*

    *They souvenired the pythonhead and came to a watering hole    Whatever beast that had drunk there before had fled at the smell of men    The men aimed their rifles at the upturned camouflage of dust*

    *They put their weapons down and picked up their canteens    Behind them they heard the sound of tunnelling, as if their attacker came from beneath the earth    The boar headed straight at your grandfather*

*They slit its belly   Purple intestines streaked with red and blue veins spilled onto the dirt and black blood puddled at their shoes   A woman brought a jar to collect the blood and cursed the men for wasting it   They scratched its flesh with knives and the dogs fought over chunks of fat   They roasted one flank and curried the trotters and someone threw the head to the excited dogs and then got bitten trying to reclaim it for the eyes and the luck of pigs' eyes   They cured one leg and set the fat in jars for dripping, then strangers came to join in the feast and someone began telling of the kill*

*Someone talked and others disagreed about the boar's last lunge and its squeal when the bowie pierced its heart   Some disputed the claim that the boar would have weighed more than a bull, that its back quills and tusks seemed bloody before the fight   But all the hunters agreed that the boar had had some ancient grudge against your grandfather, a debt unpaid from other lives   Legend said that only true hunters died hunting and to die in the jaws of a beast was to bless your sons with game and luck, was to save them from your sins*

*The boar's first run brought your grandfather to his knees   When he clambered for his rifle the boar found space to fit its teeth and tusks into his ribs   Then it stepped back to find momentum for another charge   Your grandfather bent for his ankle knife and flattened himself, spine to earth   No hunter could see enough distinction between man and pig to shoot   No hunter had time to think of a time when they could pick up their guns to shoot   The boar charged and your grandfather allowed its tusk into his cheek, gave a little of his own blood to get the bearings of the boar   Then he stabbed into its heart   The stuck pig flew up over him and landed on the knife handle and took two sure steps though dead* λ

*I remember now my grandfather in the nightstalls of Thorne Street   He was hawking a crop of oranges, their peels bruised and pockmarked, yet priced the same as meat   I kept an eye out for the quick fingers of urchins   He made two hundred rupees that night and saved the last four oranges   One for the god of the hunt, one for the god of tigers and one for each of us   I was treated to cold coffee and ladoos*

δ

I left the second Harappa   I cannot tell you what direction I took since the moon was in eclipse   I made my way forward by the dim red light the moon shone from its circumference, and by following the line of cupped candles that burned on the streetcorners and on the windowsills of houses   The street signs were curled inward, as if exposed to a terrible heat   I spun four circles then I headed in the direction that spinning had faced me

I ascended an apple tree and searched its boughs for apples, but saw only husks and cores on the ground below   I rested but felt cold   It seemed unlike a chill that could be eased by the body of a lover, or proximity to fire   I felt as if a chip of ice were travelling like a bloodclot within me   I felt it travelling up the veins of my legs, into my stomach, and gathering to itself other ice and sleet, hail and rain from within my body, stalagmites hardening on my ribs

When I was young my grandmother would often sing me to sleep or read to me from adventure books   The stories that I *remember and the songs of nonsense I can still hum were the ones she invented herself   Though years later I was to realise that the stories she told me were hybrids of fables and fairytales, of proverbs and wives' tales, I never once doubted that the seas of the moon were filled with milk, or that the sandalprint of Adam's Peak had been one night the footprint of Buddha and the next night the sole of an ascending angel   Her songs entranced me, though they mentioned the names of people and places I had never heard of and though they never rhymed*

*I sat in the tree and began to hum to myself one of my grandmother's songs about a rhino   Although I have forgotten my native language I remembered that in the song the rhino tried to fly to put out the fires of the sun, and when he fell he flattened out King Cobra   So, my grandmother explained, that is why all cobras are thick and flat, and when men stamp their feet or beat the earth with clubs to frighten away cobras they are imitating the sound of rhinos falling from the sky*

δ

λ *When the woman with hands written upon with henna left for the City of Johannes, you took your boat out onto the river* λ

*I remember I dived that day and pulled from the depths two gold bangles and a bracelet that had lost its jewel   I had only enough* pisa *for one dip in the cowtrough where an Egyptian brewed a strong liquor from cinnamon and honey   I had taken from Jolly's stall a book by the poet Nammalvar and I followed his* ananti, *his praise and love of the god who creates and destroys   I drank and read, lay back in my boat and watched the dissipation and reformation of clouds, followed the parabolas falcons made on the redgold face of the sun   I imagined the flights as a dance with the shadows cast upon the sandstone walls   The shadows seemed to be writing upon the walls   I wept and decided I would quit the Tic-Toc club, for even without her each mirror would retain her face, each hallway echo with the clinking of her coinbelt   So I came by the routine of rivers*

*I remembered the river clearly on the night I left Harappa for the second time but its name still salted on my tongue   I have kindled these words with silence and now they burn within me   I imagine that if I were to peel back my skin my flesh would be charred, my eyesockets filled with ash*

*λ Take a sip and speak, Manu λ*

*Every morning for many years before my exile I paddled my boat out onto the river   I had inherited the boat from my grandfather, who had bought it with backhand money scrounged from tarring roads and from the sale of tiger parts; its pelt for floors, its paws for paperweights   My grandfather had bought the boat to hunt crocodile but more often leased it to his friends for cruises with their lovers, tours of those monuments whose weatherbeaten walls revealed secret chambers and secret passages to the bedrooms of princes   I had filled it with earth so no thief could drag it off   I borrowed money from my father-in-law, the bookmaker, for caulking and a month of food   I gave myself as collateral, said I would make myself with fish and ferry as he had done with deals and mares*

*In the first weeks of riverwork I made fair money as a ferryman for tourists or tardy workers crossing to the paddyfields   Often the workers paid in food from their own tiffinpails or the promise of rice   The workers smelt of mud   Their pants, their cuffs were hemmed with mud*

   *Tourists sometimes tipped or left cameras in the boat   I mimed a pauper's English and empty pockets when they awaited change   I took them via monuments remarkable for the interplay of sun and chiselled stone   I toured them past holy men and holy funeral rites*

   *Once or twice I cast my net and dragged the river for fish but I soon noticed people paid less for fish than death and even the starving would spit out fish fattened on the dead*

   *Every afternoon, on the western banks, lines of people dressed in white waited for the pyre to be lit and for the funeral raft to be cut adrift   Widows were held often from the flames A man took a torch from the pyre to the raft, then another, younger man cut the moorings with a silver knife   I would follow the funeral boat in my boat, trailing a fishing net behind me   I would wait for fire to collapse the bough   Some nights, having trailed a burning raft as far as the sea, I came back to the ghats on the light of the last pyres, as explorers come to unfamiliar shores by the light of stars already extinguished*

   *I learned to wait for the moment when the ropes split and the planks came apart and had their fires wetted   It sounded as death should sound, an extinguishing   The rupee notes pinned to the shroud burnt first but I learned that I risked my own boat if I moved when the fires still smouldered   Also, if I were seen by lingering relatives I'd be owed a beating and lose my hands Yet if I moved too late the corpse would be beyond the capacity of my lungs*

   *I dived in   I searched for the split face, the body weighted*

*and disrobed by water     I wanted the coins beneath its tongue
I wanted the gold bangles needed to barter into the world beyond*

δ

*I followed the corpse out onto the river, waiting for the fire     The
twig and straw mast caught and flames the size of fingers flew
into the air and then extinguished on the riverface     I oared in
close and felt the heat, smelt the burning flesh     The float came
apart     The corpse submerged     I dived in     The shroud was like
a beacon within water     I reached it     I learnt to go down with
the body, to cut descending     I could have the shroud with a cut
at the shoulder and a cut at the waist     For the coins I needed
two hands so I held the knife in my mouth and tilted back the
cracked and stubbled skull and put my fingers in its mouth
Still I went down and felt the air burning like a lit fuse in my
lungs*

   *If I wanted the purse of coins or bangles I had to headlock
the descending body for a moment and work one-handed and
kicking against its weight     Rings slipped easily from fingers
and were often real gold     My chest tightened and I relented
with a few coins and a ring and I kicked up in a diagonal to the
white X on the bottom of my boat     I reached over the stern and
dropped my catch inside*

   *One of the coins looked like true silver, the rest were mere
pisa     The ring had a crust of red stones and a plating of gold,
which meant a week of food, perhaps good fuel     Even tin or
alloy could mean liquor or spice, and though I'm sure I traded*

*precious stone underworth, I also know I had my share of feasts on crafted glass*

*Unlike the other vultures, who needed good rain to find gold fillings at the riverbank, or other men with boats who salvaged wood and sundried it for further kindling, I was sure of a day's pay every day   My countrymen hoarded all their lives for death They schooled their sons and daughters so their rafts would float the furthest, their pyres never extinguish   Often mothers boasted of the comfort of their souls, passed around necklaces of emeralds that meant safe passage to the world beyond   An ambitious son meant peace in the afterlife, a daughter of fine virtue could buy serenity for her father with her wedding ring Hard work meant easy death, so the saying went   A deathpurse heavy as a mango could buy eternity*

*I told Dorothy that gods being gods needed nothing, and though she bemoaned the angels of rot and ruin I had called under our roof she traded hard the jewels and coins I brought home from the river   She seemed to know by facet and weight the difference between precious and stone   She said that since I wore the curse and was not blessed with sons I could have my ill passage and pocket of damn, for the bookmaker would buy her daughters into bliss*

*Once, in the public square of the city I left, I joined an audience watching acrobats   Tumbling from wooden horses onto the interlocking palms of their fellows they seemed to tread air They moved like birds and then rolled like porcupines   The apex of a mid-air starjump or free-wheeling somersault seemed like a point in infinity   At the apex the tumbler seemed like he would never fall   Recollecting now my life as a river vulture it seems as if time stopped underwater   Watches failed   Gravity slowed*

*In my memory water seems like a vacuum in which I could have
existed agelessly, where time relied upon the finite capacity of
my lungs     I imagined as I passed native blossoms whose flowers
reminded me of a crown of thorns, on the road to my second
Harappa, that I was still submerged*

δ

*λ  I followed you down into your tunnels of sleep, Manu  λ*

*I dreamed of the tomb of a king, buried in silk with gold brocade, the regal eyelids sewn shut lest he wake early     Diamond snakes coiled around his crown     His right hand clutched a sceptre of bronze and he was attended for eternity by clay soldiers, or perhaps real bodies in a disguise of clay     Yet in death he seemed made out of chalk*

*I feel this morning some affinity for all that is formless, all that is perfectly disordered, or so deeply ordered that its logic is far beyond the capacity of my mind     Chronology has stopped     I am in your company, Ganesh, having come via cities of ruin and dance, longing and silence, cities I could neither escape nor truly find*

*I moved through those manifold Harappas like a sleeper moves into dreams     I imagined myself a reader lost in the world of a book, an historian encountering with each turning page a different phase of the same city, moving towards some essence as if in timelapse, the final page an unsigned crossroad or a field with lush soil     Perhaps only a persistent librarian moving through a maze of aisles within a burnt-out library, walking amongst ashen books so ancient that their knowledge is no longer required in the modern world—the wells of Aceldama, the migratory patterns of centaurs—would one day release me from the chain of cities*

δ

*Each night I dreamt of a woman I was never to see again while I slept beside my wife    I began to hate my wife, whether she bartered her bangles for lentils and cardamom and made me king's dhal, or gave me her provocative look of forgiveness when I returned from the river empty-handed*

*Dorothy would keep my lover's letters for me after cutting out the stamps    She collected the stamps in a tin and paid them to the ayah girl as a worthless bonus, though the girl seemed to like the pictures of proteas and springbok    I'd keep my lover's letters overnight, recognising her intricate hand on the airmail envelopes    Dorothy could not read or write so I told her that a distant cousin had decided to research our family tree*

*I'd take the letters to the boat the next morning and treat myself to cold coffee and* pahn    *When I looked closely at the curlicues and strokes of her handwriting my eyes blurred and I could see walled gardens and temple walls casting shadow enough for me to place my hand against her cheek    Even after she had gone I saw in ill-lit alleys and half-lit rooms an opportunity to steal a kiss    A door ajar or a wedge of shadow seemed an invitation to brush hands, enough cover for fingers to entwine and then release    I dreamed of secret doorways within the palaces of her handwriting where, amongst other couples, my henna lover and I would be mistaken for man and wife*

δ

λ *Your father worked for the Bank of the Sun and travelled often to the City of Black Holes, which is where he first met the bookmaker    When the bookmaker moved to your district he supplied your father with a name, a number of a bookmaker in every state    Your father learned the lay of every track, studied the bloodlines of horses* λ

*My father would spend hours sweeping the dirt driveway of our house so that every pebble had been removed and sorted into a tin   He scolded my mother for leaving her underwear on the shower taps and me for leaving playing cards upon the floor   He paid our ayah girl to dust twice a day and stored his bank papers in alphabetised manila folders in alphabetised files    Yet he backed horses on chance sightings and hearings, on visionary tips revealed in dreams or by the waking world   The flight of a falcon cost us four hundred rupees when Majestic ran fourth   My mother's birthday necklace covered the bet when Cinnamon was pipped at the post    Yet his hunches also fed us and one evening paid for our home when he ignored form and omens and read the minds of owners*

*My father came home on bare feet and naked    On his back were the contusions left by stones    His genitals he covered with the vinyl satchel that usually contained his bank and racing papers    His forehead was bleeding from where he had fallen, once*

*Eight races had been run that day and by the seventh race my father had an empty pocket and an empty stomach    He had already sold his tiffin carrier and its contents, his tobacco and*

*pipe to other racegoers flush and drunk on cold coffee sold as coffee but spiked with rum*

*The horse Cottonveil was quoted at 240 to 1, the longest odds of the day    A horse like Cottonveil had no place in a race of stayers, my father later said, it had been bred to sprint in lines It had no place in a staying race unless its blood and chemistry had altered overnight    My father sold his pants, his watch, his shoes and silk shirt    He put eighty-eight rupees on Cottonveil to win and begged a cigarette from the bookmaker, the only one he trusted to pay his wins and who blessed him with each win*

*The bookmaker gave him five rupees to buy a dhoti on the way home    Pass off as a yogi at least, he told my father    Another naked man gave him a tip and my father plunged the five rupees on Hooghly Flood    Then he sat beneath the racecourse stands where he could neither see the race nor hear the call*

*The race began and the stamping, the shouting of the racegoers drowned out the hooves of horses    As they entered the straight Hooghly Flood, so my father was later told, turned four lengths in front    Cottonveil was pushed three wide and its legs had lost their form    Its tail, someone remarked, had thrashed so hard white spots had broken out on its hair*

*Every second race was fixed, my father said to me years after he gave up gambling    A punter's talent did not lie in the reading of the form or researching the line of sires    Anyone could plunge for the cut of a horse or on a whisper at the track Talent for horses lay, he said, on predicting the interests of men more powerful than oneself    Though a breeder may claim as birthright a win for his filly, or say the hooves of his new colt were made to run on clockwise tracks, my father knew the fate of horses and of the men who threw their paycheques at their tails were bought and sold behind the stables*

*Hooghly Flood slowed two hundred metres from home   Its head reared   Cottonveil caught and passed it in eight strides and beat the third norse by two lengths*

*Cottonveil's right flank was white by race's end   A stablehand met the horse midtrack and wiped it and cloaked it and led it home   The jockey changed his spotted shirt and went to stand the scales   So my father saw neither horse nor rider when he emerged from beneath the stands   He just saw his number up*

*The bookmaker touched his nose and bit his thumb, paid my father out and wished him many sons   My father found the naked man and paid the man to walk him home   His winnings weighed heavy in the satchel strapped around his neck and clothing his genitals   My father did not stop for food or clothes   He felt the eyes, the breath of younger, stronger men   Part of the way home the naked man took his clutch of pisa, his fist of Hooghly money, and ran   My father felt his followers closing*

*My father took a lead which never shortened   He knew the alleys home but kept to crowded streets   He heard the men behind him yell out, 'Thief'   A naked man was common but a running naked man fled guilt   He ducked the hands, the arms of the crowd and held his satchel tight   He thought about a rickshaw but distrusted the driver and the direction he might take   Home itself was insecure but at home he had neighbours and a rake   He did arithmetic as he ran*

*The first stone hit him between the shoulderblades, the second at the base of his spine   He neither arched his back nor tilted his head   He kept his stride   He knew then that they were a stone's throw away and by the weak force of the stone he calculated distance*

*He was a street away from home when he fell   He first clasped at the money, then at his head   He got up and continued running   He called out to our neighbour Prajit and armed him with a stick   He offered him a lakh to stand the door all night*

*My mother and I found him unconscious on the kitchen floor   Twenty-rupee notes bandaged his cut head   We stayed awake, afraid he had robbed his own bank, until he woke and told us the story*

ϕ

I extended my search thirty degrees north of Capricorn, thirty degrees south of Cancer. If, I reasoned, a banana tree could grow, however ill-formed, however miscarried its fruit, in the cold south of the New Country, then surely it could flourish a little further from the equator. The extension of my search allowed me to include the civilisations founded on the banks of the great rivers Amazon and Yangtze.

While searching for confluent rivers or divergent streams of the Yangtze I read of the Shang culture and its burial rites: the slaughter of animals and the beheading of guards to attend the dead ruler, mortars and pestles to prepare the food of the dead.

One night Mirren and I were watching a detective movie made in the City of Falling Stars in which one of the characters died a slow death after being shot by a poisoned arrow. I have forgotten the name of the movie but I recall the dying character naming the cities he had travelled to and the men and women he had loved. With his last breath he cited his only regret, that he had never revisited the Church of St Veronica, the church where he was baptised. His last words were, 'I never returned to Veronica'.

Mirren laughed out loud at the words of the dying man.

She said that she was unconvinced by the last words of fictional characters, that real people died silently or screaming, without grace or significant speeches. Others died in mundane ways, without realisation of their deaths or complaining of the stench of smoke, and she said those who died exotic deaths spent their last moments stuttering to soothe the lion or requesting a blindfold.

I laughed like a mime, holding my hands against my stomach and without sound.

I now recall the last words of Mercutio in the play *Romeo and Juliet*. I recalled that with his last words Mercutio had cursed the noble houses of the Montagues and Capulets. I was impressed that the families should remain unforgiven, for the feud had killed a noble man and from what I recall, Mercutio's curse seemed to have called death into both houses.

## Horses and donkeys

Your mother was a horse and I was a donkey. People are either of the two or the one. Horses get the attention and donkeys clean the stables. Donkeys groom the hair and all and do the hems for men to look at, so pretty pretty, and flash their teeth if teeth they have. Your mother's plaits, her *bindi* I did—who else? Even when she broke her leg I made her cast up in lovely blues and green.

ϕ

I read of the Mayans and followed a brown line into the Valley of Oaxaca. I saw the avenues of the dead intersected by the San Juan River but found in the illustration no confluence of the rivers Belize and Hondo, and the zigzag stucco sculptures of the Mayans were dissimilar to the latticework of the tapestry palace. I read of the danzantes, the dancers of Oaxaca, and wondered whether like the dancers of Caelum they danced for seduction and for the appeasement of gods. I wondered whether the Mayans with their codices and caracols, their solar charts and charts of Venus, believed themselves sole witnesses to the dance of planets, believed themselves in troupe with the sun and stars.

I wondered whether my dream city shared a history with the waking city, whether it shared dream fauna, dream natives. I wondered whether a dream road meandered through dream mountains and if this road was marked for its length by dream crosses.

The Russell Highway in the wakeful city eventually winds through the Altai Valley. Along the road small wooden crosses mark earthen graves. On the intersections of the bars of the crosses tin lids inscribed with a number have been nailed.

The numbers on the tin lids, which have been inscribed by hammer and screwdriver, begin at A1 and end at Y12. The graves mark the bodies of men and women of the native population who built the original road over which the Russell Highway was laid. A legend tells that there is a keeper of the graves, a white man who tends the highway with an axe and sack. Another legend claims that this man keeps a book in which each number has been translated into the true names of the dead.

It is a fact often neglected by the civic fathers that death marks many of our tourist sites. Tourists are never informed that male and female roadworkers, secured at night in neck braces and leg irons, died in roadside shantytowns of cholera and hunger. The imprisoned dancers of Caelum, legend says, died from lack of dance. Visitors to MacQuarie Falls or Eve's Hollow remain unaware of the men fed less than the donkeys, of the birthing women subdued with rum and told their children had died. I imagine few would dream of the snapped Achilles, the raw Adam's apple, when climbing steps to natural landmarks, but I have dreamed of their photos recording an unexplainable redness in a waterfall, group portraits where a shadow fell across each face.

I closed the book of the Mayans. Across the road a man came out of the Town Hall and took three green bins and wheeled them up the wheelchair ramp and stood them in the foyer of the building. He then came outside and locked the building with the key.

In the carpark of the Town Hall the bins are put out every Wednesday evening. Every week, when I place my own bin on the footpath, I see one of the clerks or secretaries taking out the rubbish bins. The bins are numbered 2, 3 and 4. I do not know where the bin numbered 1 has gone to. It has become a habit of mine to note the number the bins make when they are aligned, whether it be 342 or 432, 234 or 324.

A police van drove behind the barricades into the carpark of the Town Hall. An ambulance and two police cars followed. They parked and policemen and policewomen got out of the cars and set up placards that decried drink driving and drink and violence. The sirens of the police vans and the ambulance pulsed without sound. Each Adamsday, along the route of the parade, police cameras were attached to streetlights.

Each Adamsday brings a few deaths. People kill themselves by jumping into Hevel River or they are killed on the roads. Past parades have seen men kicked to death or shot over pushing into queues or insulting the Caelum dancers. Revellers return home to beat their wives. The next morning the streetcleaners wash blood and dye away.

A streetcleaner went down the street, creating tiny hurricanes of dust along the kerb. A woman in a green uniform was walking up and down the street pushing a trumeter. A man on a ladder was hanging streamers from streetlights and changing the bulbs within the streetlights. A man at the bottom of the ladder handed him fluorescent tubes of green and red. Two policemen stood side by side talking and comparing their batons. Signs warning to be cautious of the tramlines were tacked to lightpoles. A man on the lawn of the Town Hall was raking, another man was scything weeds. A woman moved between the two and placed the refuse in bags.

When I am unable to sleep I imagine walking around the streets of my dream city. I take a familiar route. As I walk I notice the birds. I name them: bloodbird, sparrow, cockatoo, crow. I see the tail of a slater disappear into a crack in the garden wall. I pause sometimes and peer into the spiderwebs strung between fenceposts, cocoons wound around low branches.

In my dream city, along the footpaths and the sandstone beach walls, across road islands and boulevards a man writes one word. The man I imagine is a homeless man and he writes in cursive with a piece of white chalk. The lettering, the colour of the chalk is always the same. The word appears amongst the graffiti beneath bridges, on the cobblestone path that leads to a private garden where a vandal had once spraypainted 'Natural Selection is Dead' and where, it was rumoured, the police found a head wrapped in newspaper. No citizen can truly say they know the writer's name. No citizen can truly say if he is presently alive or dead. The word he writes is 'Temporary'.

In the dream city I see statues defaced and the torsos of abandoned cars. I watch as a dove dislodges bricks from the charred face of a building formerly used as a bank. As I approach a bridge, which I have glimpsed but never crossed in dreams, I see a line of beggars who sit in broken-down tollbooths; some sit with placards on which are written stories. Some have lost their social security benefits and have been evicted from their homes. Some signs tell of mental illnesses and the risk of deportation. But there are other beggars who have the look of cultivated poverty. They seem clean. The rips in the knees of their pants, in the elbows of their shirts are straight and sharp. I have little money to spare in the dream or wakeful city but further along the bridge I see men and women who busk with rare instruments; oud and zither, harp and sita and I always imagine throwing a few coins to them.

I remember once when Mirren and I walked the beach towards the abandoned lighthouse of the Docker's Quarter. She was wearing a long floral dress and a bowler hat. It was a cool night and her eyes looked hazel in the moonlight. I remember that we were both hungry. She smiled whenever my stomach rumbled. We passed restaurants and cafés where patrons sat behind glass and stared at us as we passed, as if annoyed that we had interrupted their dinner views.

Up ahead of us a boy was playing with a plank of driftwood on the sand. In the boy's hand the plank of wood became a cricket bat, then a shovel. He dug a hole in the sand and stuck the wood in. Then he found a stone and an empty can and threw them at the wood. He seemed to tire of this game and he uprooted the plank and walked out into the water. In the shallows he sat down and began to row with the wood, flicking up sand and water first left then right. Again he stood up. He began clubbing the water.

Mirren walked out onto the sand and took off her hat

as seagulls flew up around her. She picked up seashells and placed them in the crown of her hat, then she placed a seashell to her ear.

I knew that the listener to seashells often mistook the echo of their own bloodflow for the sound of waves. I imagined that Mirren's circulation would have its own distinctive timbre and imagined music from the seas of her blood conducted by a moon beneath her ribs. Although my aunt disbelieved in werewolves and the antique notion of lunacy she insisted that the moon affected people in the same way that it affected tides. My aunt believed that the moon bent the lonely seawards, as it tugged seawater to meet them, and indeed in my city the abandoned lighthouse was popular with suicides. I imagined that in her mind my aunt saw jilted lovers and abandoned grooms, widows and addicts diving into a confluence of blood and water.

On previous walks to the lighthouse I had thrown stones out onto the tide, and as I followed their long, looping parabolas I was reminded of the parabolas I was taught to measure in graph books at school. Although I had forgotten the precise procedure by which I arrived at the value of X or Y, I began to think of the search for the value of consonants as the progress of a story where there is only one possible ending, where there is one true value whose occurrences are replaced by the music of numbers and where the narrator is invisible. As I write of this narrative math I recall the Book of Numbers, the fourth book of the Old Testament, and though I know that the title of the book refers to the numbering of the tribes of Israel, I imagine that the book is filled with sacred numbers: Moses entering the desert with a formula that could draw water from a rock, or rain manna from the skies. I wonder whether the seven days of the week, the forty days of Christ's exile are part of some immense, infinite formula that sets the planets in motion and dictates the daily movements of the earth.

## The life of the dance

Some gin nights I'm liking a song, Tuesdays and Thursdays. I tune to the old stations where they play the old tunes. 'Knees up, knees up, don't forget your knees up,' and I sing and laugh and while they're asleep I take off my shoes and do a jig on the carpet. Like in the Old Country I jive and how I remember when I had the boys all dancing in the halls and the bandleader Hadja Roy called me up on stage. 'Here's to Ida, the best dancer. Rock, rock, roll, everybody. Here's to Ida, the life of the dance.' That was before he became big in the films and all and Amba would get jealous and say the boys will never dance with me because you have such hot toes. But some of those boys were good-for-nothings and thought she was like a crocodile ready to eat them up, spending half the dance in the bathroom putting more oil onto their hair, you could have lit their heads for candles. But when it came time for dinner then see the start of the fun. All to and froing in the queue at Amba's pot and only Hadja Roy with that nice grey of streak in his hair, lovely nails too, coming back for seconds to me.

ɸ

When I was either ten or eleven years old I sat one day with an Advent calendar and wrote in the rectangular boxes beneath the pictures of Mary and the Infant Jesus, Joseph and the ladened donkey, my schedule for the month: clarinet lessons, hockey training, a school excursion, my papa's birthday.

I remember I feared on many Sunday afternoons and evenings the loss of the routine of days. Even when I was a child and sat watching cartoons and waiting for Sunday lunch to be served, I was aware that there would come a time in my life when the dhal would no longer be passed around the table and I would miss my late-afternoon shandy with my grandfather and Archer. Even on those Sunday evenings while my aunt ironed the week's clothes and my grandfather read the Old Testament and drank his last beers, I realised that one day the woman would disappear from the board, the reader from his book. It seemed to me then that if the few certainties of my life failed and its routines and domestic rituals were overrun by other routines, other rituals, or even just the passing of days, I would no longer have dimensions by which to know my life. It seemed to me that I could have no future if I was uncertain that the days on the calendar ahead were empty of acts I had grown accustomed to.

My aunt openly drank gin every Tuesday and Thursday night and often she would retell the story of my mother's ghost. In the Old Country my mother's ghost had visited my Uncle Boney while he was shaving. His wife heard him call my mother's name and found him on the bathroom floor with his throat cut. Cousin Kirta woke from dreams screaming of my mother. She woke with clumps of hair in her hands and eventually hung herself on a noose made from her own plaits. Other relatives, men and women whom I had never met, were said to have lost their stalls or become insane after seeing my mother's ghost. She visited the young and old, the healthy and the infirm, and she left them either dead or cursed. 'Amba comes' became a family saying. Whenever a door slammed or milk curdled, whenever another aunt was diagnosed with diabetes, or an uncle left his wife and went out wandering, it was blamed on my mother's ghost and, it seemed, when Amba came you were far beyond the help of any man or woman.

My aunt insisted that movie stars and models, even the anonymous men and women whose eyes, whose skin were coveted by others, carried their seductive smiles and graces into the next world. Some had their shoulders winged by a god and others, people like my mother, were touched on their foreheads by the bikh.

The bikh blended into the blood like vinegar into water. It glowed in the eyes of the dead who walked and glistened on thighs veiled by the sheerest muslin. The living who were bewitched by the corners of a ghost's wet mouth or by the sheen of their tongue were actually seduced by the bikh. Legend said the living should check always the base of a lover's spine, since prominent vertebrae betrayed the bikh.

No right man, my aunt argued, would mistake his own throat for his chin. No cheeky girl would darken overnight and spend hours spinning her own hair. The bikh promised flesh and love but only spelled out death.

The few coherent survivors compared the bikh to the feel of spreading poison, to being given a hunger for bad meat. Some said the bikh could develop in you a flavour for fire while others refused to speak of it at all.

By this time in the story my aunt would be drunk and would claim that my mother's spirit was cursed by my grandfather's work and she would stress that she did not mean the trade of rail. Yet when I questioned her further she would mime the sealing of her mouth with a key and then say she did not want devils rattling coins and tin cups in her dreams.

## Strange thoughts

One day when you're older you'll be wanting to do dirty things with your body and the gods know there'll be four kinds of trouble waiting for you. People have strange thoughts with their bodies and then always they'll make up the excuse of love. Out of love I squandered money and drank, what else I cheat on my wife but out of love. I was not fashioned so old to worry about vows and Hadja, because he was a man of family and reputation, brought no scandal to our bed or let it out again.

φ

I read of mythical cities: Atlantis and El Dorado, Lemuria and Lyonesse. I felt sure that in every age, in every true city lived citizens who assembled their dreams of fabled cities carefully, street by street, who fled each night from the corruption and crumbling towers to marble citadels and lush fields in which to birth a king. It seems to me dangerous to wake such people from these dreams, as it is dangerous to wake the sleepwalker, for even our current citizens dream of a fabled Utopia and group to rally for a perfect city governed perfectly and they resort to fists and weapons when disturbed from their waking dreams.

I feared for those dreamers in empires approaching ruin who witnessed the laying of lines of longitude and latitude, maps of wind and time upon the world, who sought a path to a fabled city and found none.

In my grandfather's native city I participated in feasts I have forgotten. In the feasts my grandfather and Aunt Ida shared food with the neighbours of their street and with many of the relatives who had survived or were yet to see my mother's ghost.

The neighbours sat together in someone's house in the

morning and planned the evening meal. They drank a liquor brewed from juniper and ate potato dumplings. They chewed pigs' trotters and asked who had lanterns, who had friends with coal.

At eleven o'clock the neighbours and family gathered on the street and laid the tables with whatever food, whatever drink they had bought or bartered. They were wise enough to invite the local butcher and miller, the spiceman and the fish wallah. The street, though closed off with barrels and boulders, seemed to extend to any flanking alley, to farther streets where a distant aunt or uncle lived. Extra faces meant extra ghee or pistachios, homegrown mangoes or backstep chillies, without which, they all agreed, the feast would have seemed a failure.

As one man lit the tandoor and tended the flames and tested the inner heat with rags soaked in water, another threaded the masala chicken and kebabs, the lamb chops and half-rabbits onto skewers and left the meat to air. On the street women cooked curries coloured with saffron and turmeric over barrelfires. Neighbours joined neighbours to clean the husks from corn, to knead the naan dough.

Children were bribed with small change and the promise of the setting kulfi to sweep the street, to keep the cooks full of tea or liquor. At tables people sorted lentils, musicians tuned their instruments. A few men wet the dirt street and tamped it while others set up a cardboard dancefloor. Then, while a pig turned on a spit and the curries simmered, while the ayahs stacked up plates and kept a watch for thieves, the neighbours went to sleep. They slept deep in the hottest hours of the day. They slept in their neighbours' beds or on cots unfolded beneath tables. If a man coveted the cool roof of his neighbour then on the day of the feast he could take his bedroll up there unannounced and rest. If a child longed to rest in another mother's arms then the mother was obliged to hold her. All doors were open. All property was public. Any request refused threatened to curse the feast. Any angry word would spoil the airing meat or pepper the curries with hair.

By the time the neighbours woke, the ayahs had tested the first ladles of curry and filled on meat half raw from the tandoor, burning yet not sizzling. The pig turned and beer bottles were opened. A handful of rice and cinnamon sticks, bay leaves and jelabis were set aside for their native gods.

Then, so I am told, my family and their neighbours would begin to sing and dance. The drinkers would finish the beer and start on a liquor brewed from cinnamon and honey. Songs would be requested and songs shouted down for the poverty of the singing. Men huddled in groups and told jokes about women and pythons, men who desired goats. The single women danced a modest dance for the gods and for the men who watched them dance. Skewers of meat charred yet tender were pulled from the tandoor and passed around and all were warned to replace the lids on the currypots after serving. The tables by then were covered with empty bottles, empty plates, so the later diners ate from plates balanced on their laps, though many simply drank and sang and then collapsed drunk and songless. Others danced because dancing, especially the twist, was good for the appetite. They then found themselves starving in the morning hours and went to the pots and found the pots still with a meal within.

I must have slept too deeply after a tablespoon of brandy to be awoken by the singers or the syncopated soles of the dancers, jiving, spinning on the boards. Perhaps when I awoke I was distracted by parathas and guava jelly, or was treated to a curl of jelabi, for I have forgotten whether the arms that held me were the arms of my aunt or a neighbour, or even if an aunt or uncle, touched by the bikh, held me slightly away from their bodies, scared by the resemblance of the living to the dead. I have no memory of gas lanterns or sucking a pork joint, no memory of twirling upon a makeshift stage or donkeyrides straddled on the neck of a stranger.

From what I have been told the neighbours kept indoors on national holidays. Few shared food or greeted each other on feast days of their gods. Though they traded with each other, few borrowed or lent, and to have the street always closed would hinder the iceman, the grocer and his bike. But on a whim, once or twice a year, each house opened its doors and unlocked its cupboards, each neighbour became a guest of the street.

My grandfather met Archer on one of these feast days. They had shared a plate of king's dhal and rice and sipped from the same glass. My grandfather had noticed Archer before, for who could ignore a man dressed as a clown, who slept on people's doorsteps and woke them with a chant. They sat with their fingers sometimes touching over the rice, insisting the other taste the last kebab, and Archer had told my grandfather facts.

Archer loved facts. Even on the Sunday afternoons at our home, when I had grown old enough to be allowed a shandy, he would tell my grandfather of the diameter of the moon crater Clavius—150 miles—and would name the sackers of cities, the Gauls, the Visigoths. He recounted formulae of motion and their evolution and supercedence, and he recounted the great Moghuls in order.

Archer said that when he had been a student at Vaudois he had been allowed to sleep in its library. The brothers thought it sinful to separate a boy from books, especially a boy who could talk the pride from a donkey and win them spelling bees. He read each night until he slept and overheard the brothers say that here was a boy who'd win them the next debate, here was a scholar who could bend his mind to politics. The brothers claimed to hear St Joseph's boys shuffling their notes, the turning of the best scholars in their beds. Archer however only loved books because he hated dormitories, the rustle and the smell of boys chafing their nightclothes, or crying for their mothers in the early morning hours. In the library, he could also view privately the paintings of nude women.

When Archer talked his right palm would open to the listener and move back and forth. He talked without hesitation about beheadings and the sexual atrocities of war within earshot of me, yet sometimes his palm would close and he seemed to reconsider revealing certain facts in my presence. So whereas I had previously seen Archer's hands reveal coins and doves, I came in time to believe his palms concealed a fact of history more disturbing than sex or death, a fact poisonous enough to paralyse or kill the listener.

I first learnt of the Khans and the imperial court from Archer and I watched his palms as he described the dissolution of the khanate. He said the men who followed Genghis and his grandson Kublai were unworthy of their lineage and lacked the ferocious diplomacy required to keep the empire from collapse.

One Sunday afternoon Archer convinced my grandfather to allow me a second shandy for he claimed the history he was about to tell of would gift a sober mind with nightmares. The three of us sat on milk crates while the dog and duck nuzzled our thighs for handfuls of masala chickpeas from the bowl we passed between us.

Archer said that when the conqueror Hernando Cortes made his entrance into the ancient city of Tenochtitlán, in the year 1519, his soldiers were awed by the blossoming foliage within every garden and the elaborate engineering of the canals that irrigated the ordered fruit orchards. Cortes himself admired the aviaries of the city which housed trogons and tanagers, flycatchers and heron in vast cages fluttering with tinsel and ribbon and daily cleaned. Cortes wrote to his king of the balance the city had found between the cosmopolitan and the natural, of a city that seemed '... enclosed in God's all-giving palm'.

The citizens, though meticulous with their fauna and humane to their birds, were quick to war and practised human sacrifice. When they learned of Cortes' manipulation of their leader Montezuma, they drove him out.

Cortes returned eleven months after his banishment, in the year 1520, with a larger army. He burned the aviaries down. The citizens covered their ears and noses to the stench of birdflesh, the screech of birdcry.

My grandfather clapped his hands together once in what seemed like rage. Archer shook his head and refilled my glass and that night, after four shandies, I was unable to wake myself from dreams of charred muscle and blood and bone and bonemarrow, of breasts beaten bloody against the cages—not by birds but clowns—and I wished the next morning never to hear of the other horrors of history that Archer concealed.

I once had a dream in which the library of my dream city was searched and every work of fiction, whether play or poem, short story or novel, was confiscated. The books were taken and thrown into orange bins in the city square, where, on a date to be finalised, they were to be burnt.

The public servants of my dream city had decided that the city would remain chaotic, various in the minds of citizens, if the future they had planned was allowed to be imagined by others. The difference between the planned future and the dreamed futures would be incalculable, they argued to the prince and the prince's aide, and therefore our horizons would be volatile, mercurial. The prince of the city disallowed the execution of writers and dreamers but decreed that all books were to be written on safe, allocated themes so as to maintain peace in the minds of citizens. These themes were to be sold to the writer, who could then write a non-fiction work on the purchased theme. A writer might buy the theme of jealousy, for example, and they might deal with this theme by providing in essay form a case of how jealousy had affected their dealings with a lover.

But the public servants soon found themselves breaking their own law. They found that between the unfurling of maps and the drawing of graphs came the dream of maps and graphs and the compulsion to tell of the dream. The prince's aide entrusted with the public burning woke from dreams of ashen scripts, of scholars eating the pages of ancient manuscripts. To govern against dreaming is itself a dream, he told the prince, I suggest we return the books to the shelves and hang the public servants.

When I reread the pages of my manuscript I realise that I move from west to east. My eyes move down one page and up to another in a shape that denotes rivers in the stelae of Babylon. I think I read like rivers.

## Soapstar

I will bathe in milk and like a soapstar press cucumbers to my eyes. I will sprinkle the bed with chilli powder and eat a paste of turmeric to heat my blood. I will take a star from the boy's schoolbook for *bindi* and pinch my cheeks until they redden up. Next waxing moon I will cut my wighair and hem my golden sari. In *Forever Young* Sabrina wore some lacy things for Chuck and soon she had him on her wedding bed, but where to get those things showing yet not showing your private parts?

And who has bosoms like that?

φ

I left my chair and began to walk around the library, through aisles of biography, fiction, social sciences and religion. The library is four stories tall. On the first floor is a function room where lectures and readings are held. On the third floor are offices and typing rooms, which require written permission to enter. The second floor shelves out-of-print books and the library's treasure, a copy of the Placemakers Bible. The Placemakers Bible was printed in 1562 and was the second edition of the Geneva Bible. It derives its name from a misprint, for in chapter five, verse nine of the Book of Matthew the word 'placemakers' replaces 'peacemakers'. Also on the second floor of the library are journals of early governors and explorers of the New Country. The Bible and the journals are kept under glass in a temperature-controlled room. The room cannot be accessed without a keycard. The head librarian is the only person with the keycard, though there is rumoured to be a copy in the mayor's safe. It is part of the head librarian's job to turn the pages of the journals for the purposes of viewing and to minimise the decaying effects of light and air moisture on any single page.

On occasions I have read, at the rate of a page a month, the journals of the early explorers. I have seen the faded drawings of the kaly oak and descriptions of the flight of the bloodbird. I have read accounts of trade with the native population, axes and blankets exchanged for valleys, for mountain ranges, and the Hevel River sold literally for a song and a dance.

Earlier this decade a man fossicking in the goldfields below the Rheita Valley claimed to have found the journals of Adam Gordon. He offered to the State Library three of the six journals at a price of fifty thousand dollars each. Two weeks later, the fossicker long gone, a spokesman for the State Library declared the journals forgeries. The *Phoenix* headline said that Gordon had had the last laugh on the city. The fossicker was arrested in the City of the Sun but due to ill health could not be deported.

I have not read the journals reputed to be those of Adam Gordon but legend has it that within their threadbare, rain-marked pages there is an intricate map of the migratory patterns of the bloodbird. The map details autumn flights to the interior of the New Country, describes the nests floored with bark from the kaly oak. I presume the buyers of the journals were fooled by the forger's ability to predict the mistakes of Gordon, convinced of the truth of the journals by its flaws. Bloodbirds are not migratory but common. The hoax was commemorated last Adamsday with a float of men in bloodbird drag, hawking their life stories.

Mirren and I watched the procession pass one Adamsday from the balcony of our home. People stood on the footpath below us and for as far as I could see up and down the street named after a war. One man had a trumpet while other men had drums and flutes and a woman playing a harp was sitting on one of the floats. Many of the children had whistles. By the time Adam passed us he had been decapitated. The bearers of Adam were covered in dye and one bare-chested man was bleeding from a cut above his left eyebrow. Adam's crown was tattered. His body stood on a float lined with corn husks while a woman bore his head on a pole. Behind him were drawn floats where women dressed as queens looked over men with blackened faces and black men. Children were dressed as angels or as goblins. Men passed on stilts. Women breathed or twirled fire. Batons flew in the air. I felt drunk. Mirren waved as the floats passed by. I heard fireworks, and as Adam was nearing the horizon it began to hail.

I watched a small girl moving within the crowd. I pointed her out to Mirren. The girl was dressed in rags and wore a red hat. I couldn't decide if she was poor or costumed. I couldn't tell if she was trying to escape the crowd or was lost in its freedom. She moved between witches and the legs of giants. Then Mirren pointed out the women wearing red hats, who marched behind the girl.

The women with red hats paraded every year. According to city legend they walked in honour of an assassin. The eighth mayor of the city had been a homophobe. He had called for legislature to wean infant boys from the breast. He argued that boys too long nipple fed would grow with girlish thoughts. The citizens laughed and awaited the next election when they would vote him out. The civic fathers, however, gave the matter thought. They had their legislators draw up a referendum. The *Phoenix* wrote of a groundswell, a mandate from the people.

According to city legend the assassination of the mayor did not end the debate. His diaries revealed him to be amoral, a man who withheld payment promised for sex with boys and men and who often beat his wife. His stablehand alluded to the mayor's unnatural love of donkeys.

The assassin herself was the first and last woman hung in the history of the New Country. She had had a son who had died within his cot at four days of age. Her father had been an archer who had won a bronze medal at the Olympic Games.

# I get salt

Coming across the ground is a giant who stamps the oceans and who has dust coming from his sandals to make mountains. He broke the earth like parathas into lands and then as he was having a nibble on the New Country he was disturbed by the girlmoon who was whistling to herself thinking of lassi. She was crazy for her lassi and got all fattened up drinking it becoming a ball.

The giant was also liking a bit of a drink and seeing her so delicious began sucking her dry.

Now the girlmoon wasn't liking this much for he was a giant and all and his thirst was as a giant's thirst and where can you get more lassi that late at night? So she—oh, hell, what I forgot to say was that she had the magic. Anyway, she turned the giant into a pillar of salt and blew him into the sky as stars and so when I'm making you kidney korma I'm getting salt from the stars and yoghurt from the moon.

ϕ

Outside a crowd was starting to gather on the lawn of the library and the lawn of the Town Hall. The last tram of the afternoon stopped outside the library and forty or so people disembarked and moved behind the barricades. Some people were costumed. Some children wore hats or held helium balloons. A man dressed as a warlock stood on a soapbox and began decrying the parade.

In the Old Country, in the city of my grandfather's birth, the dirt streets and the bitumen streets, the alleys and byways all lead to a marble tomb built by a king grieving for his dead queen. On his way to the railyard every morning my grandfather rode his pushbike past the marble edifice. He wore around his neck a whistle and in a blue schoolbag he carried a red flag and a white flag, as well as his tiffin carrier.

My grandfather worked on the railways in the Old Country for twelve years. I have seen a photograph of him when he was young, dressed in his uniform of cape and brown suit, brown shoes, with his long eyelashes like moths' wings half covering his eyes. He is staring directly at the camera.

When we arrived in this city my grandfather applied for and was given a job on the railways where he worked as a ticket collector. The railway workers of my city have shorn heads. It is the law now, but when my grandfather worked on the railways the underground was unfinished and the job was still seen as respectable. Nowadays commuters avoid the trains of the underground because of constant electrical breakdowns and rat infestation. The commuters distrust the workers and distrust the inaccurate neon schedules beside the ticket counters. Many of the workers are ex-prisoners. Many are said to live beneath the ground. Some are employed to travel down into the dark tunnels with masks and poison gas and are paid forty cents per rat. The commuters have also come to believe many of the city legends about women being left in carriages unhitched at abandoned stations, or stations under construction where the travellers were ordered to disembark and told to wait for a connecting train that never arrived. Legends are told of trains that travelled along routes where all the placenames had been removed, the commuter relying on memory alone as they passed through unnamed suburbs, hoping the doors would release them to a familiar platform somewhere along the line.

I feared train travel even in my childhood when the trains ran above ground. Once or twice I travelled with my grandfather to the tip for car parts, through suburbs whose names may be interpreted as the Spring of Horses or the

Burrough of Saints, and I saw into the backyards of houses where men and women were screaming at each other while their underwear swung in circles on the clothesline and into alleys where I feared murderers of children lurked. I feared the gangs of boys who waited at the rampmouths of stations, sharing cigarettes and whistling at girls. I feared for my clarinet. Even now, on nights when I see the trains passing through the station of my quarter and see the lines of lit faces, or the profiles half hidden by newspapers, I imagine the commuters travelling to a place which will be the last destination they reach alive on this earth.

I remember another search I conducted many years ago. I had read a story in my grandfather's *Reader's Digest* about a man who had spoken to God on a CB radio. From what I remember the man in the story was an ordinary, lonely man who lived in the City of Bridges but who, in his wanderings through the airwaves, had stumbled upon the frequency of God. Doubting that he was truly God, perhaps believing that some jester was perpetrating a hoax, the ordinary man asked God to prove himself. God promised to submerge the continent of the New Country under an inch of water for a full minute. God arranged a time. God submerged the land.

I have forgotten how the story ended, whether the man questioned God further or if God became impatient with the man's disbelief, but for a week after I read the story I believed I would find in the written histories of the New Country the historical intercession of God. I searched for records of wetted plains and submerged crops and in my mind I saw coastlines emerging from the water, translucent fish birthed by the seas upon beaches. Yet I could find no record of the event and it was only after I questioned my grandfather that he explained to me the story was a work of fiction.

Along the street named after a war the police were arresting a man for throwing stones. A death truck had passed along the street and the man had found some stones on the lawn of the Town Hall and had pitched them at the truck. Others had thrown dye and corn and abused the drivers. They then abused the police for arresting the man and the police pulled their batons and waved them at the crowd.

Once a week I was awoken by the sound of the death trucks that searched the city streets for stray dogs. It was rumoured that these dogs were rabid or carriers of disease, that they jumped at children and at women for their food and groceries. I had seen many of these dogs, thin and brown, sometimes toothless or without tails. They scavenged on roadkill and learnt to upturn bins. They were harmless, it seemed to me, just hungry and sometimes excited by the scent of meat.

Two men drove in each death truck, the driver and the armed hangman. Bullets were only wasted on the larger dogs and crazed. The hangman carried a long pole. Each pole had a noose which could be adjusted by a lever and a strap to fit the neck of any size or shape of dog. The dogs were caught and shoved into a cage of iron mesh. The cage sat on the back of the truck. Ten or twenty dogs could be squashed into each cage. They were taken to the pound. The cage was lifted off and set beside a pool. The dogs were kept for three days. They were neither fed nor watered. The dogs fought. Dogs lost ears and eyes to other dogs. Carcasses were fed upon. On top of the cage was a large metal disc. A large magnet picked up the cage by the disc and dropped it in the water. A charge was then sent through the pool. Within a minute the dogs were cleanly dead, the cage then cleaned. A city legend told that the blood and flesh of the dogs was used as feed for cattle. Another legend told that we ate the dogs in our pies.

## Pepper

All I needed was to give him one of my flashing looks with a little glitter on my eyes to get his pepper up and set his mind along one track. I took him by the hand and we went inside the fridge. He unravelled me. Cool yoghurt on my back, between my thighs. Bottles falling and cartons and his breath I could see. His tongue between my bosoms.

ϕ

I came across cave paintings in my readings, stick figures beside waters and migrating bison whose thick bodies were depicted with a thumbprint of ochre. The river was often a zigzag.

I faintly remember, or perhaps I have imagined, a child's drawing of a family. In crayon on a large sheet of butcher's paper, a child, perhaps a classmate in kindergarten, had drawn a father, a mother and two small children. The line of people receded in height from the father to the youngest child, who was a little girl. The girl's dress was a red triangle. Her hair was a dark curve. The father was wearing a black hat and carrying a brown box which I presumed to be a suitcase.

Though I cannot remember when I saw the child's drawing, I presume it was years later at Antioch High that I saw an ascending line of men in the pages of a textbook. The shortest of the men was brown-skinned. He was hairy and hunched over. He was holding a stone. He was more monkey than man. I understood as I looked at the illustration that each man in the ascending line represented a phase of humanity, an evolution. As the line ascended, the hair receded from faces and the implements refined from flintblade to axe, from sword to arrow. The spine of each man in each incarnation straightened. The skin lightened. The final, tallest man was carrying a suitcase and wearing a bowler hat. He was white and clean-shaven. He seemed to be smirking.


One afternoon, after Mirren and I had returned from the beach, a large bloodbird flew into the shopfront window.

The window retained the shock of blood. Mirren put her hand over her eyes. I went outside.

The previous spring a pair of bloodbirds and their chicks had nested in one of the trees on the grounds of the Town Hall. I would hear them every morning when I brought my manuscript out onto the balcony. Sometimes I still hear them, when they interrupt my recollection of dreams. The call of the adult bloodbird sounds like the word 'kraal'. Legend says it has lost its song. The bloodbird is omnivorous and survives mainly on berries and fruits; it is also found commonly around the dogbowls of our quarter in the late afternoons, nibbling the leftover dog meat. Naturalists claim to have found the skeletons of lizards and smaller birds in its nest, once even the remains of a human ear. The bloodbird, however, does not have the equipment to kill. It lives on carrion. It derives its name from the deep red plush of the underside of its wings, and on dark afternoons in my quarter I am sometimes shocked when I see a tongue of vermilion in the branches of a palm tree or when I see the underwing blaze as it swoops upon a discarded morsel in the street, its blue crest standing upright and resembling a tuning fork. Five years ago a virus which began in a species of bird was transmitted to humans. The virus was linked with the bloodbird. Scientists surmised that some homeless man or woman had eaten the carcass of a bloodbird and had caught and spread the virus. It proved fatal to a dozen elderly asthmatics and caused fevers and nausea among the younger citizens.

The bird twitched on the ground before me. Mirren came out and stood beside me. She seemed to shiver. The wings of the bloodbird were tucked tight into its body. I hovered over it. Its eyes were flat and black. Mirren said it was stunned. Its beak was crushed and blood leaked from beneath its crest. The crest was the colour of lapis lazuli. The bird's ribcage expanded and contracted. The crest seemed to brighten as it breathed.

Though I knew that the feathers of the carcasses of birds that I saw on bitumen roads were dulled by weather and wheels, I preferred in that instant to believe that the colour of a bird's plumage left its body with its breath, that colour drained from its wings like blood.

Mirren went back inside and brought out a chair. She sat beside the bird, which twitched again when it saw the chair. Mirren said it was too fragile to touch. It seemed a touch would kill it.

When I think of the word 'fragile' I am reminded of the night of a lunar eclipse.

I watched my aunt drinking gin from her coffee cup by candlelight that night. The radio was playing some song that always reminds me of khaki men running into gunfire on the shores of a beach once named Kalliopolis. I was allowed to stay awake to watch the moon clothed in earth-shadow. I could hear my grandfather talking to himself in his sleep. He was muttering, 'Ma Sympathy, Ma Veil', words I recognised, though most often he sleeptalked in his native language. My aunt had been drinking for over two hours. She had filled her cup to the brim and would refill it after every sip. She put her face every now and again close to the halo of candlelight, as if to sip there as well. She got up from the sofa, holding the bottle close to her stomach, and the candle cast her shadow against the wall. As her hips swayed her fingers drew two small circles in the air. Then she extended her forefingers and parted them. Her left hand swung left when her hips swung right. Her right hand swung right when her hips swung left.

Her shadow moved as if it were her partner and its darkness seemed to deepen as the moonlight faded.


Mirren sat down. The bird tested its wings. It shivered and called but it seemed to have lost the talent of flight. Mirren blew at it, as if her breath would compose it. I looked at our reflection in the shopfront window. In the reflection we looked as if we were in between the pillars of the Town Hall. People passing in cars and trams stared at us.

Mirren said that when she was a young girl she was a good mimic of the cries of crows and seagulls. She said that one summer she had even perfected the call of the falcon. When she was young she spent many summer vacations at her maternal grandmother's in the Gassendi Valley, which is a few hundred kilometres north-east of her native city. After the death of her elder sister, Maya, her parents became fearful and superstitious of the house where their first daughter died. Mirren's mother claimed she saw Maya in nightmares swinging on a tyreswing with her throat slit. Mirren's father complained many mornings of visions of Maya: Maya burnt at the stake, Maya shot by a thousand arrows. Yet Mirren travelled often to the house of her grandmother, eager she said to face whatever ghosts awaited and hoping for snow. As Mirren talked I imagined two young girls collecting nettles beneath a fir tree, where the ground was re-emerging from beneath a covering of snow.

I imagined one of the young girls, a girl I was later to know as Mirren, picking from the ground an egg with brown spots and holding it in the palm of her hand. I then imagined the girl remembering a map of stars as she stared at the spotted egg. As I write of that daydream I remember how the dark whorls and knots in the woodgrain of my grandfather's bookcase reminded me of the rings of Saturn. Years later when I learned of the implosion of stars I saw black holes in the whirlpool grain of the bookcase, and I dreamed of trees holding within their trunks a blueprint of galaxies, forests containing maps of universes as yet undiscovered.

In this last year when I have listened intently to silence, I have begun to think of sound as a landscape. I recognise in sheets of written music—in the peak of the semiquaver, the ox-bow lake of the treble clef—horizontal maps of a country I have yet to discover. I have imagined a landscape that emerges from a horizon of notes and I have dreamed of travelling this landscape and finding along my way a perfect note to rest within.

As we sat and waited for the bloodbird to fly Mirren told me of the secrets of magicians. She had worked with many kinds of magicians in her life, from young men who simply pulled pigeons or rabbits from their sleeves to masters who could levitate, or vanish on a whispered word. She said she spent most of her worktime ironing or sewing panels into their illusory hats. She showed me with her hands the shape her body assumed within a basket pierced by swords and described the sliding glass panels of the cage which hid then revealed the hippo or elephant. She talked of the last magician she had worked for, a man who performed tricks beyond any of her explanations. She said he had once made a bunch of roses disappear and neither he nor she could explain where it went. One night a volunteer from the audience cut her hand on his sword and the magician put his hands on hers and stopped the bleeding. The magician stopped working after that, Mirren said, for he felt he had no control over the gift he had unearthed.

As Mirren talked I looked again at our reflection in the shopfront window. I saw the reflection of the bird take flight and soar across the road to one of the trees in the grounds of the Town Hall, and yet when I turned around the bird remained in its box. I looked again into the pane of glass and I saw that the box in the reflection was empty. Mirren said the bird was dead and sang to it in her native language.

I kissed Mirren on the forehead. I reflected upon the flight of the bird's reflection and persuaded myself that what I had seen was a trick of the light, or a mirage of some kind. I persuaded myself that I mistook the flight of another bird for the bird in the box. Bloodbirds are common, I told myself.

# Pickles and kisses

What ugly funny things they are custom to do here. Just like home these feasts are all expense and waste, Daddy has that one thing spot on. But you can't help but laugh when the head falls off. Once I saw this man Adam in the city, all bronzed up. I am not liking the city even in the day, but where else to get cheap shoes? Anyway he's got a nice cut about him and lovely wavy hair like a filmstar. But those darkies godhelp look like they're born in coal and you'd take them for part ape until they dance.

So my bald Jacky said to me on the next feast day of Adam we'd take a bottle of champagne and sandwiches but I said gin and parathas to see the fun. I'm saying there is so much time to pass beneath the bridge till then, why can't we have an outing now? And of course he has one kind of excuse or two like every man—because his daughters would be upset and he has his business and tries to hush me down with pickles and kisses.

φ

*I have, it seems, left that world over which the maps are thrown like nets   I am free from the weight of divining instruments—barometer, watch—whose daily prophecies dull awakenings*
*Am I dead?*
   *λ I cannot answer, talk on λ*

δ

*My third Harappa seemed to be a land of two dimensions Houses looked like the drawings of houses, the landscape of landscape paintings*

*I was reminded of the boxes of tea in the pantry of my mother's home—Darjeeling, Northern Rivers   Each box printed with a stylised depiction, rice paddies in a rudimentary blue and green and a brown worker resting a pot on her headdress   Tea houses passed by a man in a bowler hat   Harappa seemed a city that existed only on a teabox   Harappa seemed all facade*

*Yet I found true north in the third Harappa, for I saw the counterglow and coordinated the sky   Reconsidering my journey I estimated my route as a parabola that cut through the edges of three Harappas   I neither placed myself nor found comfort   I knew I was moving and moving forward if only by degrees   I thought perhaps I could still navigate toward Morning if I could find the cross made by Turies and Avior, Koo She and Markeb*

*As I neared what I interpreted as the border of the third Harappa I saw a city of tents, their highpoles bearing one-colour flags printed with the names of planets: Blue Jupiter, Black Mercury   I neared them and smelt fresh dung and sawdust, saw deep, unfilled holes nearby a cluster of balloons*

*A roulette wheel loosed from its table turned quarter circles in the wind   I saw three men on the horizon practising highjumps over a low bar and heard the music of cymbals, then a roaring crowd*

δ

λ *The eyes are infinite    All landscapes, battles, people and loves can be recalled    Close your eyes, remember bells* λ

*My wife never wanted Ida and Amba to sew    If they know to read why should they sew, she said    Let their ayahs sew    I was given an old sewing machine by a club widow returning home and I had repaired the motor and replaced the needle    My wife repaired my shirts and trousers    She bartered samosas with the Samvis, the local tailors, for scraps of silk and our dhobi took in their washing for a week for thread    She planned to make a new sari for Amba and a skirt for Ida but Amba wanted a shirt she had seen some filmstar wearing    We could not waste material on fashion so I brought back the funeral shrouds of Brahmans from the river, as they were never burnt*

*Amba watched her mother though her mother shooed her away    She watched the semicircles of her thumbs around the pulsing needle    She watched her adjust settings and reset the spools of thread in the bobbin    I watched as well but misunderstood the intricate dance between foot and arc of hand, could not read the quick fingers and the intent behind the sewer's eyes    Within a month Amba had woven her shirt and then with Ida's help they made gaudy, ill-fitting skirts and shorts without pockets and began selling them in front of St Gregory's    The parishioners bought their clothes, though the thread unravelled at the crotch and hems    Perhaps they liked the toil and cheek of my girls    Perhaps because the girls were not beggars they singled them out for charity    Cloth is cloth    The Lord helps those who help themselves   They were bringing money into the house   We had mutton once a week*

*I wanted for Amba wealth and good bones, temperate blood and sons   When I touched her head for the first time, felt the soft shell of skull, I felt something within me yield   I felt as if I had resisted love up until then   I trembled, thinking of any crossroad or misstep that might have led me from their mother I trembled thinking how fatally they could have missed their own conceptions—the trainwreck my father walked from, my grandfather unarmed in the domain of tigers   The line once split can never heal*

δ

*One night the Tic-Toc club held an egghoppers dance for visiting engineering students from the University of Dreaming Spires They had come to build a bridge   On the driveway of the club as I was coming in to work I found an invitation   The invitation was addressed to Joe Mann   I had on my waiter's uniform of white jacket and black bow tie   I nodded to Sabu at the door   He was a younger man than I and was not paid by the club   He stood at the door hoping for tips from members and their guests He arrived every evening in his self-made uniform of white cotton with a purple sash that stretched from his shoulder to his waist He wore an ornate scabbard and knife on a belt around his waist On quiet nights I often saw him pruning the vines that coiled around the pillars of the club with the knife   The knife, he once told me, was an heirloom from his great-grandfather   It was gold-plated and was worth more than his house*

I showed Sabu the invitation and he laughed   He asked how it came to have my name on it, if I had written it myself   I said that one of the students simply had a name that resembled mine and the handwriting was finer than my own

I saw men in tuxedos smoking and clinking glasses and heard the stories and gossip women with bare shoulders and long legs told to one another   The women had high-pitched laughs and wore jewels around their necks   Some were dressed in saris and wore intricate bindi that laced around their foreheads and resembled the glyphs of an ancient language

I went through the back doors into the kitchen which was full of smoke and the smell of frying eggplant   I saw my lover and she slowly blinked her eyes   Chef Govinda was pouring batter from a large tub into a frying pan and as the pan filled my lover cracked an egg into the middle   Govinda had once been burnt in a kitchen fire, so his face looked sewn together from the skin of other people   He had a goatee beard and a tattoo of a goat on his right bicep and he refused to make goat curry, even for colonels and cricketers   He claimed a goat had saved his life, though he never told the full story

I rang the dinner bell and began serving   I served from the left and picked up from the right and my lover followed me with a pot of eggplant sambal and spooned a serve upon each egghopper   The students looked confused   Some broke the yolk and ate the egg but left the pancake   Others rolled the whole pancake up and ate with their hands

A band played songs which I had heard my father singing: 'Quel Marlene' and 'Knees Up Mother Brown'   Over time the balloons descended from the rafters and were popped by the *heels of the dancing women   I felt uncomfortable drinking from the half-filled glasses printed with lips   I drank from the men's glasses while they swayed against each other or fired champagne corks at the dancing couples   Bottles were passed amongst the dancers   My lover asked me to steal her anything from any one of the dancing women   I heard people splashing in the pool*

*Between the tables and the kitchen I sneaked leftovers into my mouth and what I could not eat I emptied on the back step for the three stray white dogs that lived on the grounds of the club   One of the dogs was three-legged, having been shot on the last dogday when other strays were exterminated   The dogs barked and snapped, bit the cakes and licked the step for egg*

*I stole a packet of cigarettes from a table and took a box of matches from the kitchen and I went outside to smoke   The revellers had begun a game played with pen and mime   I went through the front door and Sabu asked me if I was enjoying myself   He asked if I was the guest of honour and I smiled even though I hated him for a moment   I saw a small boy approaching along the driveway   Sabu waved the boy away   I knew what the boy wanted   There were shoes to be shined inside the club*

*I blinked as I approached him   He was naked except for the dhoti around his waist   I saw his eyes when he walked into the lamplight   I looked him up and down   He was silent   I blinked again and looked into his eyes again*

*I estimated that I had been roughly the boy's height when I was his age   I had worked as a shoeshine once   We shared scars on the bridges of our feet   I asked him to show me his palms*

*He asked payment for this   I grabbed his hands and he*

*screamed   I turned his hands over as he wriggled   His palms were as smooth as my own and without lines   Who are you? I said   Who is your mother?   Who are you?   When he claimed to speak no English I asked him again in Hindi   He pointed to my shoes   I shook my head   Then he began to walk away   I couldn't follow him   He stopped   I called to him   I offered him a place of trade for his name   He said his name was Roy*

*I watched the boy with the box for the rest of the night   My lover asked Govinda to fry fish for the boy and fed him parathas and lassi   She stroked his head and said he could have been my son   His mother's name was Pria   He didn't know his father*

*The revellers threw coins at him as they passed   He tried to follow them   He chased them on his knees, begging to let him shine   One reveller pushed him away, thinking he was asking for more alms   One woman pinched his cheek and he mumbled a curse at her*

*I put off the lights in the ballroom and cleaned the trestle tables   A man who looked like he was made out of shale was asleep in the middle of the dancefloor   The chef wiped up his workbench with his apron and took a long swig from a brandy bottle   We found a purse which we left with Sabu*

*The boy counted his money and made pillars out of coins in front of his box   Seven pillars of even height   He gathered one pillar in his hand and offered it to me   I shook my head and closed my hands around his and the coins   My lover and I waited and watched but never saw him again*

δ

*Lord of Hosts, where is the book that tells of all consequence?*
*Where is the book that tells of the divergent road or route, the*
*decisions left unmade, the words left unsaid?*

*Often I imagine that men and women are in orbit in this*
*world, that the movements of their minds and bodies can be cal-*
*culated   Commuters travel in peaks and troughs to central*
*places populated in certain hours then abandoned at later times*
*Totes are made for births and deaths   Patterns of migration, of*
*spending are graphed   We fall amidst a million general lines*
*But where is the book that calculates difference?*

δ

λ *Your father cleared a debt with your marriage   Dorothy was*
*born with a harelip and never went to school   Your father had*
*lost his bank job and you were owed a dowry   So the bookmaker*
*and your father arranged a deal that squared your families up*
*and the bookmaker promised a lakh to the gods to bless Dorothy*
*with sons* λ

We were married at the racecourse in the City of Black
Holes   I was brought into the betting ring on a painted elephant   The bookmaker met me at the door to the service with a
jar of honey and underhanded gold   While the priest recited a
mantra from the Yajur-veda the bookmaker led me to the altar
The coins clinked in my pocket   I counted them over and over
between my fingers, since Dorothy arrived an hour late   She
rode in on a white horse flecked with brown paint   She was
dressed in an orange sari   Her veil was threaded with real gold
I was wearing the tuxedo that became my uniform at the club

*Even during the ceremony, during the expression of wishes, the bookmaker spoke in hushed complicity to my father His quiet leanings distracted me from the eyes of my bride Everything he did, it seemed, whether buying a book or his favourite kebabs, was a deal done with undertone and sealed with something extra for your health, your sons*

*The reception was held high above the track in a banquet hall where dignitaries and cricketers, princes and movie stars had danced and drunk The bookmaker blessed the children with coins of chocolate and coins of gold and tipped waiters in scotch bottles He pressed champagne upon track officials His son had poured beer into horse troughs and he and his friends had lit the tail of a donkey with firecrackers and slapped it on its rump The fireworks drew the guests to windows to see the fun, though some mistook it for gunfire and hid under the tables*

*The scotch, the champagne was gone by the time of the wedding toasts So the bookmaker mixed into jars a cocktail of rum and gin, of mango juice and soda, and had the waiters set a jar at every table He called for glasses to be charged and raised to Dorothy and me and the guests charged their glasses and sipped Some grimaced and others spat the potion out When I called for them to raise their glasses to the father of the bride and thanked him for his hospitality and the hospitality of the track, they raised their glasses all of them but few sipped again*

δ

*Steers ate the wreaths Their slow jaws ground petals into a mash that purpled their tongues A cowherd tapped their hind legs yet they remained at the feast of flowers   Out further men were sifting knee-deep through ashen water for gold and silver teeth, for chains and rings which rain had brought towards the shore   Vultures hovered nearby*

*A man stepped forward to wetted fires and split the charred skull of his father   Many could ill afford the funeral raft and so corpses burned in pyres on the shore   Others wanted a jar of ash to keep for mantelpieces, or to sprinkle at the foot of icons within holy ruins*

*I heard another's head explode in the flames   It made the sound of a popping cork*

*I had planted at my daughters' births mango trees for funeral wood   They were green saplings at Amba's death, useless even for kindling   Her death bankrupted us, even though I bought cheap wood and laid out nothing for the gods   Laying out gifts for the gods to ignore and for men to steal, I told myself, was like throwing salt upon our grieving house*

*I wrapped Amba in her shroud, sprinkled her with lotus petals and a country liquor   I placed her in my boat, which was lined with blocks of dung and wood   I touched her head with saffron, then turmeric*

*My wife invoked Rama for Amba's safe journey and wished exile upon my soul and upon the soul of my father   Only a black father, she told the sky, would feed her children with bikh and death, only a dog of storms would bark black heavens down upon her roof*

*I tried to push the boat out but it stuck in mud   I pulled it by its bow with a rope   As it drifted past me I struck a match and threw it in*

δ

*Nothing lingers like Amba's absence   I dream my body retains her handprints, the printing of her lips   I dream my chest, my cheeks printed with her fingerprints   I see her body at thirty, her face at forty   I see her married and pregnant each year with sons*

*I see her face in mine*

*If only the mirror could collage its faces, the river retain its reflections*

*I remember once I smashed the mirror of our bathroom cabinet   The cabinet door was ajar and a box of talc was falling out and I went to catch it   There was blood on the glass where it cracked and blood within the cracks that splintered from the point of impact   Glass fragments stuck in my knuckles and blood was running to my nails   I washed the contusion and disinfected it with iodine then I dried and bandaged the wound*

*Then I sat and started to imagine where a child of mine could cut or graze themselves, where in my house were there nails to catch on skin, or coil of heat to burn   I feared hot oil and the brace of the gas heater, electricity and the stranger at the door*

*I locked up everything   The front door had three locks and a cast-iron and mesh door   The windows were locked from the inside and pieces of wood were jammed between the locks and sills   The fridge was locked   The water heater was chained and locked   The cupboard had a chain around the handles   Each night before the opening of tins and jars we unlatched and unchained the cupboards*

*Yet, Lord of Hosts, my thieving cursed the water used to wash my Amba    As her child grew I saw her in his every gesture*

*I lost all time and words for him    The shape of his mouth, his expressions of fear seemed a mime and shadow of Amba    He muted me with his eyes which were his mother's eyes which were my eyes and my mother's eyes*

*Even Dorothy said his veins would flow with bikh, that he was born with a taste for death    The bookmaker touched the boy once with his lucky thumbs and begged the heavens to relieve him of his halo of evil stars, to forget his pariah heritage    Then he threatened me with a cane beating if I ever brought the boy's black luck beneath his roof*

ϕ

The tragedian Livius Andronicus translated the works of Homer into Latin, and while looking for his birthdate I found a photograph of a mosaic. The mosaic depicts St Ambrose and it was here that I first learnt of the man whom the church of my quarter was named after. St Ambrose lived from 340 to 397 AD. He wrote hymns and prose and was credited with originating plainsong. In the mosaic he stands before a background of blue tesserae. He wears a beard and has large ears.

The keystone of St Ambrose's Church is engraved with the words 'PRSVR Y PRFCT MN VR KP THS PRCPTS TN'. On the day of my grandfather's funeral I entered the church and noticed a partly restored face amongst the faces of a mural.

When I think back now I imagine the restorer of the mural finding the face of Christ beneath the layers of dirt. I imagine him polishing, cleaning further, bewildered as the paint flakes, the beard and cheekbones disappear. Below the face of Christ, I imagine, the head of a prophet, his mouth agape, his hair plaited with rivermud. I imagine the restorer continuing to uncover with his brushes, his cloths, deeper faces in the surface of the wall. Finally, after a lifetime within the company of pigeons and priests, when his tools are blunted and the wall concaved, he finds his eyes level with the eyes of the blue god.

I walked up to the front pews and sat beside my aunt and Archer. I looked over my shoulder at the pews full of men and women. I looked past the people and out through the church doors where strangers were walking or alighting from trams. I imagined that the mourners within the church were arranged in a line of intimacy with the dead, as the parents of a bride and groom are seated closest to the altar, so that behind us were first cousins, then second cousins, followed by friends and acquaintances. Within the mind of each mourner, I presumed, would be a story or fragment of a story from the long story of my grandfather's life, and if I were to be given access to each mind I could piece together, like the placement of tesserae in a vast mosaic, some rough portrait of the man. I imagined further that if I held my eyes close to this mosaic and saw into the pores of stones and within the facets of fake and true gems, the colours of the stones and gems would break the banks of their rough diameters, colours would spill in waves and these waves would cast shadow enough to conceal lovers in private gardens, streetnames in imagined cities.

Last year in my city a casino opened. Mirren asked me to accompany her to the opening but I declined. The casino is called the Celestial City and though I have never entered through its glass doors and ascended its escalators to the gaming rooms and rooms of merchandise, I have heard Mirren and overheard other gamblers remark upon the star-shaped chips and the dice games named after planets, the Moon Bar and the Sun Bar where a patron can buy a milky Einstein's Mo or a Galliano Galileo.

Mirren returned the morning after opening night. She smelled fresh but looked tired. She wore no makeup and had covered her eveningwear, the velvet dress and matador's vest, with a coat she bought on her way home with money she had won on roulette.

She walked straight into her bedroom after her return and when she re-emerged hours later she asked me for a cup of peppermint tea and offered to buy me dinner. As she sipped her tea she told me of the dream she had had the night previous. In the dream she was sitting naked at a blackjack table and she was dealt a hand of cards. The cards were from a pack of the Arthurian tarot, and as a circling wheel of lights spun at the edge of her sight and a man called out, 'Snakeyes,' Mirren slipped the cards between her fingers and revealed Spear Two and Stone Two, cards whose divinatory meanings contradicted each other. She called for the third card and the dealer, who had turned into the Grail Hermit, dealt her a photograph of her sister Maya. In the photograph Maya was four years old, swinging on a tyreswing. Mirren showed her hand to the dealer and the dealer paid her out in fake jewels. Earlier in her dream, and then again later, the casino had become a labyrinth where she had baited a minotaur with blood-soaked towels.

From the back of the pew in front of me I picked up the pamphlet for the funeral service as the priest walked to the lectern. On the last page of the pamphlet was a photograph of my grandfather wearing a frayed white suit, the only suit he owned, and a tie, which on its reverse side had a drawing of a girl wearing a grass skirt.

The priest stood at the pulpit and began to address the mourners. He talked of the movement of life and the soul that accompanies that life and of the body as the vessel for the soul. He talked of migration and the migration of souls. The priest said that here was a man who had seen war and poverty, the loss of a wife and the death of a child and yet came to the New Country believing it to be Eden, came with a fire in his heart. He said that the angel of death moves amongst us each day, each night, and that men and women stave off death by their children and their children's children, all of whom carry vestiges of the departed, and though it was natural to mourn with the family of Joseph Manu we should also celebrate with them, for the soul of Joseph would be carried up to heaven on the wings of angels, for the Lord is our shield and buckler. He then pointed to where the body should have been, at the urn of ash from the burning of the hands, and said, 'See Gabriel, see Michael attendant on the body to heaven.'

When I think of the word 'soul' I see in my mind a tambourine which exists physically within the body, so that when the priest committed the soul of my grandfather to the care of angels I imagined the archangel Gabriel carrying to our Saviour a wooden circle rattling with tiny cymbals.

I dreamed that if within each man and woman, each girl and boy, existed a tambourine which collected for each lifetime, each incarnation on this earth, a cymbal the size of a coin, then a man or woman or girl or boy could draw from their chest an instrument by which all their lives could be pulled congruently into music. They could rattle on those precious spheres a tune which would reveal to the listener all their desires and regrets, all their loves and deaths, and this music would recall for the musician of the soul all lives led in worlds now forgotten.

This morning I dismembered my clarinet. It lies in the front room on a cloth. Beside the cloth lie earbuds, newspaper, matches and a chamois. Normally after I have cleaned the fingerholes and polished its brass I reassemble the clarinet and light a cigarette. I blow smoke through the mouthpiece. The smoke filters from the fingerholes, as if it were the visible soul of the instrument. But this morning I held the keys in my hand and dreamed of Mirren's body. I dreamed that Mirren lay on top of me. I placed my mouth on hers, touched her palate with my tongue. I laid my fingers on her spine. I fingered her vertebrae. I dreamed I played upon her spine a note that echoed in the imaginary landscape of music that I once sought. I dreamed our bodies curled within a treble clef, her tongue quavering over the staves of my ribs.

I was sure I would one day seduce a woman with my clarinet. I dreamed of the reliquary where my jazz would hide her clothes. When I attended Antioch High I hid from the playground ricochet of balls and insults in the music room. Though for a few years I played hockey with the school team I made few friends amongst my classmates. At presentation nights and school assemblies I played solos on my clarinet for the gathered audiences, but I like to think of myself as someone whose name could not be recalled after the final day of the final year, neither the fastest nor the slowest runner, being neither the brightest nor dullest of students, unremarkably punctual, neat.

Aunt Ida has told me of the rivalry that existed between the two great schools of her native city. The students of Vaudois and St Joseph's were famous throughout the Old Country for their manners and their dress, their scholarship and feats upon the sporting fields. Parents sent their boys and girls to board, in separate dormitories, with the nuns and brothers of the schools. The parents were promised a child who by the end of their schooling would not cross a street without first looking to help another, who would say a rosary for every foul word or disrespectful thought. The students of these schools would be assured of clean work, clean nails. They would wear their grooming, their courtesies, as if they wore halos.

Yet Vaudois and St Joseph's kept no charity for each other. For two hundred years they had exchanged blows in the boxing ring and goals on the hockey field. It was considered a sin to marry outside your school. Unpolished shoes, unplaited hair, theft or sex in uniform brought curses upon your school and blessings on your rivals. Legend said that when one of the old schools fell, all of the Old Country would fall with it, so the students of Vaudois and St Joseph's were told that they knotted the whole of society when they knotted their ties, that they kept the streets orderly by keeping their margins straight.

## Salted tongue

When he's done he goes the colour of salted tongue, like all the blood has gone from him. And his breathing goes so heavy that he almost neighs. And he'll turn his hand to any trick, like ones I learnt from Archer. But hopeless at dancing with two right feet and soon I said we need a bed when our pepper's up. He's a sweetie though and is giving flowers for me, magnolias.

ϕ

After the priest had finished speaking Archer stood up and went to the pulpit. I heard his shoes tap against the stone floor. He tucked his shirt into his pants and adjusted his suspenders. He smiled. He went and stood behind a large

Easter candle. He clicked his fingers three times. He fanned his fingers out behind the flame. The candlelight cast his fingers against the back wall of the church. He entwined his thumbs. I concentrated on the shadow. The shadow took the form of a butterfly. The butterfly turned into a boat. The boat sailed on a river. The river turned into waves of an ocean. Over the ocean flew a bird. The shadow bird perched on the tabernacle. On the tabernacle the bird turned into a heart. The heart then grew wings and the shadow disappeared.

I looked back at Archer. He had begun to cry. His makeup ran in rivulets down his face. His face looked as if it were dissolving. I imagined that if he continued to cry his skin would be washed clean and his skin then flake to reveal flesh, and his flesh would drip from his bones and his bones powder.

I have seen Archer crying in a dream. He had taken me to the zoo in a city formerly called Al-Tierra. I was eight or nine years old. He was wearing a purple suit with brown buttons and a wig of green dreadlocks. The cashier admitted us for free because she thought he was a clown. The zoo had started a breeding program for griffins. The griffins were housed in a fenced-off field about the size of a football oval. Invisible nets hung a kilometre above the cage. A bridge traversed the middle of the field, high above the fledgling griffin cubs and their attentive mothers. Visitors to the zoo walked the bridge and stood and watched the griffins from a height. The visitors were sealed in by glass. The male griffins were kept elsewhere, penned in and tranquillised, legend said, because they ate their young.

Archer and I stood on the bridge and looked down. People either side of us had binoculars and cameras. We watched a suckling griffin leave its mother's teat. It stumbled across the grass. It flapped its wings. People began shouting at each other to look, to watch the first winged course of the griffin. Cameras flashed. The griffin stood still. The mother covered her eyes from the flashbulbs. I looked at Archer who had turned into a griffin. Tears were running down his face. He said we should go and talk to the manticores.

I cannot truly recall all the instances of my day the night I dreamt of griffins, but I can account, even at this distance, for some of the images in the dream. Around the age of eight or nine I became obsessed with mythical beasts and read whatever book I could find on minotaurs and lamias, on the sasquatch and the monkey-king. My favourite book when I was a child was a book about the feats of Hercules. The book had illustrations of Hercules cleansing the stables and slaying cannibal birds. In one illustration, Hercules, muscles bulging from beneath his bearskin, was holding a woman's girdle.

When I think of Hercules now I do not see in my mind the drawings of him in the book. Before I remember the drawings I think of another drawing which I saw in the advertising section of my grandfather's *Reader's Digest*. The man in the ads had formerly been a skinny man with glasses but after only three months of using an exercise machine called the ChestBender he had acquired a physique that attracted women and frightened bullies.

Around the time of the dream of griffins, Archer had

newly arrived in the New Country. Perhaps in my mind the cannibal birds, illustrated in the book of Hercules descending upon a lone fisherman on Lake Stymphalis, became the griffins of the dream. Further, in the zoo of my city there is a lion enclosure about the size of a hockey field, through which runs a bridge, and I had often walked with my grandfather across that bridge and watched the bored lions lying prostrate on the small grassy hills.

I once read of Gondal, a country that existed only in the minds of the three Brontë sisters. The three sisters travelled Gondal and wrote poems and stories about it. I could never find these stories or poems but I imagined myself a tourist to its dark moors and its six-month winter, a connoisseur of its provincial chocolate, its spring water.

At the end of each summer on the moors of Gondal, in the years before their extinction, I imagined the soft earth thudding with the feet of migrating centaurs. I imagined the bronzed torsos, the grey and black fetlocks disappearing towards a dusky horizon, witnessed only by four citizens of Gondal. But soon the centaurs were forced to flee the nets of men who hunted centaurs for their potent blood, their lucky tails. The ribs of centaurs were powdered as an elixir for impotence, as a mascara for thin eyelashes. Hooves were sold as paperweights in bazaars. The carcasses of centaurs killed for sport and profit rotted in our minds. Though zealots dreamed them, though troubadours recorded their great bravery in their songs, all that remained was the memory of centaurs and a notebook of the sisters which recorded habits of their breeding, patterns of migration.

δ

Afterwards, outside the church, a man on the other side of the street was looking through a lens, which was attached to a tripod. I presumed he was surveying the street. Another man was taking a photograph of his wife in front of the church. As the flash flared Archer walked between the man and his wife. The man cursed. Archer apologised and offered to photograph the couple together. The man looked at Archer, his face veined with tears, his absurd funeral suit, and smiled. He handed the camera to Archer who took the photograph, and while the camera flashed I thought how forever that man and woman would have a photo of Archer between them. I dreamed that a child of theirs in years to come, sitting with a photo album on her lap, would question her parents for the name of the clown.

## Shedding my hair

I am shedding my hair for Jack Macquarie and rubbing his bald cream head. I am on fire for him. I make him kiss my back, the back of my thighs. Not but for the days of Hadja Roy did one man see my wighair off but I'm telling him of all the things of Amba, and how I pulled my hair and then had no need to pull it since it fell like leaves. He said who is he to talk, his hair fell from wearing too many hats, no wonder his wife took off. Then he put on the wighair and laughed and laughed, till I thought I was having a *butcha*. I kissed his forehead.

ϕ

In an archaeological textbook Ea, a god of the Phoenicians, was carved into the four corners of a stone watertank. He held a water jar. Ea was a god of rain in the time of Sennacherib, and though he interceded between heaven and earth he had no earthly love, his hands never sought or touched the brown hips of a well woman or fell upon a body in a field of barley.

If, as one scholar wrote, he had loved the goddess Anat I feared for him. Her altar was smeared with henna and her womb was fertilised only with blood.

In a fridge in the staffroom of the library I found a crate of bottles labelled 'mead'. I opened a bottle and poured the mead into a glass. I drank the first bottle in gulps, as if the bottle would soon disappear. The mead had an aftertaste of cinnamon and honey. I opened another bottle and took it out to my workdesk.

By dusk the crowd had spread onto the lawn of the library and on the lawn of the Town Hall. People were jostling each other and leaning over the barricades. At my feet were books opened to pages marked with other books. One pile was as tall as my thigh.

I read of stupas and ghanats, and pondering the underground tunnels of the Persians wondered whether a meeting of lover and azure king could have occurred below the earth, by the banks of an underground stream. Perhaps Darius met Mithras beneath the plains of Persepolis. Indeed she was a goddess of the earth. But by then my eyes were tired and became unfocused from the mead and work. Pages of tombs and kings, columns of writing and keys to maps turned before my eyes. Constantly I tilted my head forward and rubbed my temples.

I imagine that there is a moment in every search of any kind when the searcher loses faith in what they seek. Looking forlornly over deserts and seas seemingly without end or, as I did, reading of those books I had yet to consult in bibliographies, the searcher begins to question the value of what is sought. Unlike others whose quests might have promised rain or fire, immortality or the removal of sins, I sought only a story, whether it be true or fictive, and the character of that story, whether he be god or man. I would have been content last Adamsday to find even a glimpse of this blue divine and his paramour, lovers who seemed blessed in a jungle where bananas were plentiful and the river foliage gave up garlands, birds surrendered feathers for the god's crest.

## The fare

Darling Amba, sweetie, you are with me. Sweetest are you among sisters and loving your son like he was my own.

Baby Amba in the candlelight, come with me now and with my pink Jacky bald and he'll chip in for the fare, Amba.

ϕ

Nowadays when I remember my grandfather's funeral procession, I place Mirren beside me in the taxi. We follow the hearse in which my aunt and Archer sit with my grandfather's ashes. I hold Mirren's hand.

The procession arrives at the Necropolis near sunset. To reach there we pass a racetrack, before that suburbs whose names could be read as the Valley of Spring or the Valley of Glades, and earlier still we pass through streets named after wars and explorers, war heroes and poets, having left the church at an hour approaching dusk.

The procession travels past the kosher butcher and the library. The hearse leads us beneath the railway bridge where the radio in the taxi goes dead. When the transmission resumes I hear my grandfather's voice saying, 'Ma Sympathy, Ma Veil', and I explain to Mirren how I plan to imitate my grandfather and abstain from words and elaborate foods. As we pass the Bar Panther I tell Mirren that I hope to inherit through abstinence the words, the stories my grandfather withheld from me, and I tell her that I see her face whenever I say or hear or read or write the word 'love'.

The Bar Panther went through many takeovers and renovations before becoming the pub that Mirren and I drank at every Saturday evening. It was once a sandstone building with wooden tables and listed sailors and prostitutes as its patrons. At that time it was called The Survivor and its walls were hung with driftwood and lifebuoys said to have been salvaged from the wreck of Adam Gordon's ship. In time the bar was taken over and legend says that the so-called historical treasures, the brandycask driftwood and rusty ship's wheel, were left outside the renovated hotel in a skip. The new owners called the bar Rita and the Snake, referencing the legend of Ludwig Rheita, who was said to have found the Rheita Valley by following a trail of snakeskins. The owners decorated the bar with rabbit traps and picks, with telescopes and snakeskin couches. On a hatstand in one corner they kept the explorer's incongruous bowler hat and the barman's joke was to tell patrons that Luddy was in the loo.

In another incarnation the bar became the Hero and Donkey and was frequented by war widows, by soldiers returned home. The bar offered half-price drinks and fry-ups to all who wore their medals or the medals of their fathers. Many begged or borrowed medals and bankrupted the hotel.

The pub then became The Pauper's Rest, then The Bloody Coast. For a month before it became the Bar Panther it was called The Melting Pot. I drank at The Melting Pot one afternoon and the bargirl told me the legend of Paolo and the tunnel.

In the days when the bar was called The Survivor a young sailor from the Land of Fire met a prostitute named Chloe. They shared a chaste four-week romance before the sailor was called back to sea. Paolo said Chloe had his mother's eyes. Chloe thought his body had the shape of the sandalwood statues sold on the beach by immigrants. On the docks the boy sailor promised Chloe to return, promised to dream only of her in the years or decades before his return. Chloe promised Paolo to see his face on the faces of her clients, to mishear their drunken groans for his promises of marriage, promises of wealth. Chloe had been promised marriage and wealth before and was dumbstruck when, two years later, Paolo returned.

He returned bearded and with two falcons tattooed upon his wrists. One falcon was named Law and one Disorder. He boasted to Chloe of the money he had won dicing in the City of Perfumes and remarked upon his ability to outeat, outdrink any of his shipmates. His skin seemed to have wizened, as if salted and soaked in brine.

Paolo said he was a man who kept his word and expected his word repaid. Chloe left her trade. They had sex in alleys that stunk of fish, in rooms where junk was stored. A fuck on a park bench put a crick in her neck and a splinter in his cock. When his winnings withered he pimped her on the docks and put on a show for a circle of men.

Chloe wanted her true Paolo and doubted the returned sailor thick with hair. She tried to trick him with questions of the places they had years ago made love and he scolded her for the test. She asked him once to open her front door and he plucked the key from a cluster then fucked her on the threshold.

Chloe could no longer see a difference between the chapped hands of her sailor and those of other men. His body like theirs arched away from hers in intercourse. She hated him and held him. She wished him drowned yet loved the story of his return. The sailor had returned a different man but he had returned; though his promise had turned to vinegar it was still a promise kept. His breath smelt of cigars and his hair had straightened and fallen from his temples, but his eyes seemed to her still like the green of leaves withdrawing for autumn, his fingernails seemed still like moons unripe. He was a stranger as he'd always been but not the stranger she'd imagined.

The first publican of The Survivor brewed a liquor said to leave the drinker blind yet thirsty. Legend said he had a tunnel made, a tunnel to hide the still and the distillers, a safety route in times of raids. Legend said it was sealed by later publicans, to be found only by an empty bottle tapping for the hollow in the cellar wall.

Chloe loved her story and foresaw a bad ending. Two regulars, the publican and his son, said they missed her gin-and-coconut breath, her milky tea served after sex. They said they knew a place to store a body. They found the tunnel and dug it out. They found a crate of wine. They found some tubes and mouldy bottles. The tunnel stank of piss and strychnine. Potatoes had gone to powder in a hessian bag.

Chloe bought a round for all. She laced Paolo's rum with strychnine. She watched him gulp and ask another shot and die.

Over the years, over the incarnations of the pub, customers have complained of moaning or remarked how the sea sounds like a dying man. The barkeep then tells the story and sets a rumglass full upon the bar. No later owner, the barkeep says, can find the hollow. Paolo's body insulates the space.

Mirren scoffed when I told her the story. She had heard the same a thousand times before. Every public house had a residing spirit. Every publican had a tale to tell of love and death.

Mirren replied to my story with a story she claimed was retold nightly in every hotel of her native city.

Once, returning from his job as a surveyor of deserts, a husband found his wife in bed with another man. Enraged, he struck at their skulls with an ancient axehead he had brought home from a bazaar. When he calmed and saw the bodies half dressed in a garment of blood, the skulls hollowed in, it seemed to him another man had puppeteered his body, had clenched the jaw and bid the hands. He therefore reasoned himself innocent.

He considered deserts and could see a hundred caves and pits, plains and vistas where the lovers would disappear within a month of winds of sand, where a trail of blood would be concealed within a minute of his passing. He also knew he would never reach those dream reliquaries of blood and bone with his cargo of slaughter.

So the surveyor of deserts looked over his native city and thought of the pulse of water beneath the earth and considered the welling and the emergence of the pulse. He dismembered the bodies and sought rivers.

Often the drunken narrator of the story, in the shadow of the bar lights, would wink his eye at the listener and claim the lovers, piece by piece, were reunited at the confluence of the Volga and the Don, though any native schoolchild could debunk the story. Many have claimed to know the man who found the woman's head, to be a distant cousin of the fisher of her arms. Some have even pointed a wicked finger at a sleeping drunk in a corner of a pub and named him as the killer, free for lack of evidence. Lovers elope, the courts were told, axes are tuned to kill and ancient axes are dyed with blood.

Mirren said she had grown up with the legend, had dreamed the wailing of the lovers, mistaken riverlogs and rivershadows for arms and hair. The legend continued even when the lovers returned as tourists, the fiction retold to the source of the fiction.


The night after my grandfather left for the town of Morning I came home to find Aunt Ida hiding beneath the kitchen table. She was holding a string of rosary beads and a bible, her knees drawn up to her stomach. I looked around the kitchen, fearing a rat or a stranger. She waved me towards her. I went in under the table. My aunt mimed horns and a tail and whispered the name Satan.

She took the rosary beads from around her neck and placed them around my own. I looked around.

I knew that the Devil was legion. Besides Satan himself, there were Mephistopheles and the Golem, there were subdemons and apprentices to Satan, and further there were the devils of the radio and car engine, of the clock and batteries. The pilot light within the stove was itself a devil. Gas could be seduced to the bidding of Satan.

I looked upon the floor for cloven hooves and a barbed tail and I clutched my crucifix and wished for holy water.

Then I heard the call of a kookaburra.

My aunt screamed and began a mumbled prayer. She said a devil had come with wings and eyes for her. She screamed to Christ a pardon for the wanting of a child.

I managed to coax my aunt outside after relinquishing the crucifix and arming her with a knife, which she blessed with four repeated psalms of the Valley of Death, then with four chants in her native language, the language she claimed to have forgotten. I pointed to the kookaburras which had perched on our roof. I said they were lost. I said they were probably the pets of one of our neighbours that had escaped their cage. Though wary, my aunt put out a plate of breadends for them. The dog ate the bread. I told her that kookaburras were carnivorous. My aunt claimed to know the tune of the song of Satan and claimed to recognise its issue from the throat of the bird. Yet she took next a bowl of chopped liver outside and held it up to them. She said that in the end any bird was a bird of God and only He knew the song's end and the true pitch of the song and its corroboration in heaven. The duck came and stood between her legs. The dog nudged her until she fed him some of the liver. She handfed him and he licked her palm. The kookaburras called and flew away and my aunt covered her ears, dropping and smashing the bowl, and the dog licked the remaining liver from the shards of bowl.

$$\delta$$

I hope one day to conjure the memories of what I have imagined rather than what I lived of the day we buried my grandfather's hands. Though we reached the Necropolis at dusk and placed the urn in a small plot marked by a bronze plaque, though my aunt threw in her crucifix after the urn and Archer took off his orange foam nose and placed it also in the ground, I hope one day to remember Mirren's hand upon my shoulder as we stood on the banks of the Hevel River and emptied the ash onto the riverface. I hope to forget my aunt and Archer's drunken lovemaking that night and remember Mirren and I walking along a secluded goattrack leading from river to road.

Last night I woke from dying. I dreamed of drowning in a river and being resuscitated moments after my death by a child who was a stranger to my waking hours. All I now remember of the child in my dreams is that a stylised sun was tattooed to her left ankle.

I tried to remember how I came by the river and I tried but failed to pair it with other rivers I have seen or read about.

I began to believe that my death in dreams was only a signal for the death of the dream itself. I imagined landscapes where dreams may be buried. I imagined drought-stricken plains where dreams could be evaporated through fissures of the earth and gardens whose trees and plants were rooted in dreams; hyacinth flowering from the third submergence, magnolia germinating as wings tire in a dream of flight.

I mused that just as the citizens of my city were buried in public cemeteries and the basic details of their lives recorded tersely on tombstones, so were their dreams commemorated in botanical gardens, as if trees and flowers were markers on the graves of dreams that thrived upon the city's dreamers. If I could have chosen in my waking hours the tree that first took root when the child put her mouth over mine, I would have chosen a kaly oak.

I once read that the poet and painter Dante Gabriel Rossetti had exhumed the body of his wife Elizabeth so as to recover the poems he had buried with her in despair. I imagined that my dreaming exhumed the child in my dreams. I imagined that her body lay fossilised deeper than my dream of her. I believed that just as the spirit leaves the body after death, so did her body leave the body of the dream upon the opening of my eyes. I was tempted to believe that she could only live on my temporary death.

φ

Mirren disappeared in a dream. In a dream Archer made her disappear. Before that he had undressed her with his wand. She had stood in front of a white sheet, the silhouette of her body facing the audience. By a wave of his wand and a twitch of his powdered blue face he removed finally her sequinned bra; before that a body suit hemmed with stardust, a tutu, firstly a blond wig that covered her red hair.

Each of the audience members seemed to be performing an act or wearing a disguise. I stood beside a ventriloquist whose slack-jawed dummy was repeating the words 'Mare Crisium, Mare Nubium'. Another man was eating fire. Twins in tuxedos were singing a Blind Dog Harvey song.

I assure myself it was a coincidence. Perhaps that night as I lay asleep, as, according to city legend, ghosts came to dress in candlesmoke, I heard drawers opening and closing. Perhaps she had come into my room and whispered a farewell and her whisper had infiltrated my dream, for the next morning I awoke to find Mirren gone. The legend of candles on her worktable had guttered and stones and shells had been spilt over the table. The drawers were empty. Two odd shoes were under her bed. Costume jewellery lay in an open box.

I went out onto the balcony and hoped for a storm. I thought that if she was alone on the city streets a storm might force her home. I could hear the tide coming in on the shore and could smell the saltwater on the wind. Many afternoons when the shadow of the Town Hall darkened the street and I saw cats scurrying under stairwells and awnings, I would sit out on the balcony and watch the gathering grey clouds and wait for rain. I liked the feel of the rain washing through my hair. I liked to close my eyes and feel raindrops against my eyelids. I liked to imagine it was washing off a disguise. Although I knew that meteorologists could explain with charts and instruments the formation of stormclouds and map and name the winds that drew the clouds over my city, I imagined that the sea, whenever it was bored of its cycle and eager to venture inland, conspired with the wind to form rain.

The night before the radio weatherman had foretold a maximum of 48 degrees. Barbecues were banned, citizens were encouraged to wear hats and sunscreen. The elderly were told to stay indoors, in shadow. Drink water, the weatherman advised, avoid sport and other physical pursuits. Businesses had opened by 6 a.m. and closed by 10. By 7 a.m. extra trams were sent to the lines leading to the Anchor Quarter. The front-page headline of the *Phoenix* read 'Scorcher' and its editorials predicted death by heat stroke, shortages of water. Bakers, foundry workers were given the day off. By 8 a.m. there were women on the street wearing cut-off shorts and bikini tops. Men walked about shirtless.

The morning started and remained cloudy. The sunlight was sporadic enough to be mapped patch by patch. Beachdwellers covered themselves in blankets and seemed yet to believe in heat. Citizens along my street came out of doors and looked up and returned indoors quickly, as if the sky were only bluffing, and the sun would soon be out.

On the evening radio news the weatherman said he was baffled by the wind shift, the evening rain. He talked of the vagaries of weather, of instruments duller than the human nose. He apologised to the chilled beachdwellers, the elderly hospitalised with colds. No one could have foreseen, he ended by saying, that the sun would disappear. The sun was hot, he said, but shied its face from us.

Mirren did not return.

# Pestlesong

Oh, Lord who has crossed time and rivers
Why will Jack Macquarie not come to eat?
See this paste is drying
And the pan is hot now
Why will he not come to his place at the table?

ϕ

Late into my search Last Adamsday I looked at the tapestry again. I had been searching, because of the banana trees in the foreground and because of the distinctly eastern appearances of the cornices above the treeline, for stories in equatorial countries and leaning towards the myths of those civilisations: Sumeria, Babylon, founded on rivers or systems of rivers. But then I noticed what should have been instantly apparent to me, a gash of vermilion in the palms of the banana tree. I followed the line of half-concealed wing, saw the crest bent like a banana for courtship. Though the body of the bird was hidden I named it as bloodbird. I wondered whether the weaver in some elaborate joke had seen a parallel between the myth of a country that lay between the tropics of Cancer and Capricorn and a myth of the New Country, found some conjunction between the kaly oaks on the banks of Hevel River and the shelter required by the god in the act of seduction. I was convinced then that the paramour was a resident of the temple in the background; certainly the shadow of the turret fell across her face and masked the true colour of her eyes.

I realised that I was no longer searching for any landscape that existed in the world in which I write but a landscape formed within the mind of the weaver, a landscape perhaps assembled on her travels or gleaned from an imagined journey and fleshed out by her reading of other ages, other cultures. I could no longer trust that the lovers were from the same myth, or the same race, or even that they were of the same country or continent. Perhaps, I argued with myself, the weaver had matched lovers across centuries, across races, and suddenly it became clear to me that the jungle canopy may not only have provided refuge from the eyes of a suspicious father or jealous husband, but also from the eyes of history, from time; and the lovers, impossible and sacred, existed alone in the world of the weaver's mind, where cultures had condensed for the time of a solitary kiss.

Certainly the lovers could never be found, the brief confluence of their bodies never disturbed by the turning of pages, if they could not be found on maps of ancient or modern worlds, or even in the mind contemplating those maps.

I half closed my eyes and daydreamed about the artist of the tapestry. She was sitting alone in a room which grew darker as I dreamed. Her callused fingers were speckled with blood, her eyes too half closed. I followed the rhythms of her crewel needle. I watched her bloody fingers threading even after she fell asleep. I dreamed that she also worked alone, pausing from her worktable only to make her simple meals, and occasionally to dance. I failed with my scant knowledge of needlework to know of the intricacies needed for the headdress, to have it slightly tilted, as if it would soon fall. I did not know if the background was threaded out first, or the foreground, but I dreamed that one day she chanced upon a story that reminded her of her own courtship, her own braceleted arms, her own forlorn look as she came to know love and the debt of the heart, she had felt moved to depict in detail one moment of it, one scene.

I was half asleep when a bugle roused me to the wakeful world. The Adamsday parade had begun to pass.

## Stormdogs

So he didn't show his face, I won't waste my gin on worry. With my colour and my glitter eyes so many men want to put their eyes on me. But may a meteorite hit his shop while his daughters are splashing on the town. I have more ways than one to pull stormdogs onto his roof. Not tongue, not the heart, have any bone. I learnt the good of English so quick quick who'll not say and hold their peace that the heart can't start new. So many dreams have left my body I'm longer not of need to waste my gin.

ϕ

I crumpled the last page of notes I had written, pulled a table over to the window. I put the chair on top of the table to see over the heads of the crowd. I saw a boy throw a satchel of dye. The satchel burst over a man on stilts and I remembered rain.

Within the length of one night's dreaming it rained on the graveyard for forty days. Down the cement path of the graveyard water spilled and the gutters overflowed and the Isabella Lawn was swallowed in mud and new flowers were uprooted and washed away. When the rains ceased and the water subsided I found four drowned rats and a child's shoe without shoelaces. Weeds had begun to sprout at the edges of graves and vases overflowed with brown water. The bark of the kaly oaks was blanched and the bark of the eucalypts was stripped. The icons seemed dull and grey.

The parade passed before my eyes, dancers and mock slaves, giants and clowns. They passed each pane of glass as if moving through a triptych, as if the windows were a canvas that had loosed its figures. Batons flew and dye burst upon bodies. Men wrung the sleeves of their shirts and women dusted their skirts and the revellers drank from bottles sheathed in brown paper and others bought food from vendors. People danced and children cried. Gods wheeled by in cornhail.

A group of boys stood at the entrance of the library. They pushed at the doors and tried to ply the doors open. They gathered some leaves and sticks from the library lawn. They made a pile of the sticks and leaves and one boy lit a match and drew it close to the kindling. The flame did not take. The other boys circled the kindling. Then someone from the crowd screamed at the boys. The boys ran. A policeman came later and kicked the pile away.

Men in green and gold robes were walking on their hands. Women in the fashion of the twenties and thirties passed by in Jaguars and Rolls-Royces. Diamonds sparkled on the fingers of the women, feathers blew upon their hats. A man dressed as a duke clutched at a fake wound in his chest. Firecrackers turned figure eights in the sky. Catherine wheels spun in blue and orange, in circles of red and green. Flagellants, dressed only in loincloths, smacked cat-o'-nine-tails against their backs. Ahead of them walked monks holding lanterns, police with shaven heads, and the women wearing bright red hats.

I looked down at the dancing clowns. They mimed the eating of corn. They pulled at each other's genitals and danced a figure eight. They slapped each other on their behinds and pulled down each other's pants. I failed to recognise Archer among the clowns.

Four men pulled a float carrying a golden donkey. Four other men dressed as sailors pulled a boat bearing a mermaid. The crowd threw fake money at the mermaid and someone threw a toilet roll. A couple were kissing up against a lightpole.

In line then came the city totems: a falcon and a dingo holding between them the city crest, then a dugong and a seal. The Anchors were represented by men in blue overalls, their pockets stuffed with salt. I heard so many songs I failed to recognise any one tune. Men and women marched in uniform for Bride's Hill and the men and women who died in war. Gypsy revellers, in accordance with tradition, wore tarot cards of the minor arcana upon their foreheads. The forelocks of a line of rabbis were plaited with white and blue thread. Dwarves paraded. Paraplegics hung streamers from the handles of their wheelchairs. Railway workers paraded dressed as rats. The fireworks continued. A man dressed as a crescent moon and emblazoned with the name of a hamburger chain threw boxes of cookies into the crowd. People fought over the cookies. His foam moon suit was speckled with blues and greens. Men came dressed as manticores, women came dressed as lamias. The mayor and the towncrier wore tattered clothes and had lost their hats. The crowd quietened as the music for the dancers of Caelum began to play.

The dancers of Caelum danced as kangaroos and as the hunters of kangaroos. A woman became fire and raced through the dancers pursued by a man who was wind. Always throughout their dance either the soles of their feet or the palms of their hands remained upon the ground, even when they mimicked flight. The dancers' penises were drawn as snakes. The dancing women had breasts painted purple. The crowd unravelled from the barricades. They dropped their corn and dye. Some gathered their children within their arms and left to follow the parade.

## Eye on

These men here have no shame. Now the postie is saying you have a lovely garden, you must have green thumbs. And then he says what a shame for that man and his shop leaving the street. Well, I told him never mind, who's to know what mischief that man caused and softly softly I'm thinking to myself I could have danced in films with Hadja Roy, let him pack up his things and run like a blind mouse. Then, thinking the postie's got his eye on me, I say, *Cana*?

ϕ

I returned to my desk. The towers of books had collapsed and pages had lost their markers. I had forgotten which books I had consulted and which remained unread. I picked up a book and tried to concentrate as the people whistled and a trumpet sounded but the words on the page before me seemed disconnected from one another, as if freed from the lines of print.

In illustrated histories of the world I saw the bojongleurs, forerunners to the troubadours, who could mime or tell a story while they swallowed swords or juggled balls. I saw the great Alexander weeping before maps of the known and finite world, his lover's hairy fist gripping his right shoulder. I saw illustrations of feudal lords in trade with barbed-tailed devils. I saw Dresden's upsidedown map of the world. Nowhere amongst the legends and never amongst fable or myth did the name of the god and his consort appear, and as the last revellers disappeared from my view, I felt sure that next Adamsday would lack this god.

I flicked through pages of later civilisations but it seemed to me that empires after Christ were informed by reason and doctrine, the residing gods of the home and the forest, icons of the life and afterlife were purged and burned. My god, the weaver's god, could easily have been lost in those ashes. Scriptures of the moon and sun became palimpsests for the Word, however prophetic of the Word they may have been. I dismissed those later countries sacked by guns and missionaries, their rivers running blood, I dismissed those dark ages, those revolutions, simply by closing books.

I remembered, however, that in the folklore of the Old Country it was considered taboo to destroy or defile the manuscript of a scribe because every work contained part of the soul of the writer. To harm the work of a writer was to harm his or her soul. To even step on a book or handle it roughly could bruise the soul of the writer.

Recently I heard a writer of fiction claim that many of his characters were based upon people he knew, that he had stolen aspects of his wife, mother, friend and son for his work. I considered whether the legend of the Old Country originally read, or should be amended to read, that a book contained the essences of many lives and so to tear or burn a book was to injure the souls of a family, a race.

I came to then wonder if I had witched into this journal an essence of Mirren by the act of writing. I became afraid. Whereas other men had held Mirren's body in their hands, had traced the parabola of her breast and run their palms over the clusters of freckles on her thighs, I worried that I held in my hands a precious aspect of Mirren, without which she could no longer be called by her true name.

Therefore, knowing I could not destroy the journal, I went back over all I had written, dead civilisations and still-flowing rivers, gods and lovers, and I replaced her true name with the name Mirren.

As I stacked the books in front of me I remembered a belief I held as a child. I believed that books were no longer published, that books were antiques that the adults in my life had inherited from their parents and their grandparents. I believed that at some stage in human history, men and women had decided to stop writing and publishing books. All of the authors on my grandfather's bookshelf were dead. I believed that books were reliquaries of an ancient knowledge, a knowledge to be hidden from a young boy's sight. For a child to read the books of adults was to place themself in jeopardy, like staring directly at a solar eclipse. I felt part of an ancient society when I first began to read the books of the adult world. I doubted that any of the children in my class were privileged to have access to the world of the dead.

However, one girl in my class at primary school seemed to have travelled further than I into the world of the dead, and to have suffered for it. Her first name was Tara. I have forgotten her second name. She claimed to have read furtively from the encyclopedias of her mother about the travels of Marco Polo. She always misread and mispronounced the name Polo as Polio. She believed that Marco Polo suffered, as she did, from a disease that required him to wear a brace upon his leg. Yet, Tara told me, despite his brace Marco Polio had charted many new worlds and had been in his life a trader and cartographer, a translator and a lover of queens.

I remembered then something which Archer had told me when I was a child. He told me the people of the Continent had once debated whether the dogmen of the Old Country could be converted to Christianity. The people of the Continent believed, in the time before Polo's travels, that the people of the Old Country were elegantly dressed dogs who stood around barrelfires discussing what empire next to pillage, and yet, as Archer told me, the Old Country had by then survived invasion and the rivalries of emperors; Moghuls had fought wars east and west of holy rivers. The ancient currencies of the Old Country showed kings as the slaughterers of lions; reliefs on temple walls depicted lovers in acts of sodomy, acts of dance.

Perhaps I lingered too long on pages of other lands, lingered amongst those civilisations whose dress and customs were immediately foreign to me, because I hoped there to recognise something far beyond myself. Perhaps I hoped there to discover a truth I had been unaware of, or to find myself stripped of the disguise of centuries. I admit I neglected the country of my birth until after the end of that night's parade. I admit I averted my gaze from what was before my own eyes. The god *Kṛṣṇa*, ancient of ancients, is blue as an adult, blue as a child. He is the lord of the mace and discus. He is both god and lover.

# If

So you go on with the life of living, nothing eaten, nothing gained. Small *pisa* life is not knowing the day from the night and who's to know that man of mine may return and what a *jhap* I'll give him and maybe show him Archer's map of bruises. Then he'll know what threads attach him to gods above and gods below. Anyway, the postie wants to put his eye on me, why else would he waste his time around my house with his thick lips talking—lovely day mishus, lovely dress mishus—and on a gin night? But who's to know I'll sell the house and if the boy comes home with his flute between his legs in his bed he'll find a stranger, nothing less. I'll go home and if Hadja Roy has one good leg we'll dance and gin our days away and find four ways to splash out on the town.

ϕ

*Leaving the third Harappa I began occasionally to see numbers within words    At first I thought my eyesight was failing, that my eyes adjusted poorly to light or fine print    But then in stop signs I saw the number eight and I misread memorial stones and public notices    Even when I tried to recall passages from the Bible which I had memorised years before, I saw in my mind's eye the dre8am of Nebuchadnez7zar, the fl1ire next ti0me*

δ

*The bookmaker had a price and fix on all things except grief   He
called me a coolie and saved his money for the living   I'd rather
feed a fortune to the goats, he said   They are not there whom
you seek   He claimed Dorothy after our Amba died, claimed she
was repayment for his grief   No pariah could console a mother,
he said   He'd further trust a horsetrainer than the son of a low-
born dog and offered the gods an honest lakh if I were to die in
pain   He wanted increase on my father's debt since I was less
than sticks to him and had bent his mind to personal dealings
when it should have stayed trackside   He'd barter back my
name and sham our deaths if I took Ida and the boy and left
His daughter could tend his ayahs and accept his neighbours'
songs of loss   Perhaps due grace would get a card of darkies
home or consoling jockeys leak a word or two   He did not need
our ghosts to linger round and blight his stories   Take the fare
and leave, he said*

δ

*Even from my house of exile I wrote a weekly letter to the
woman with henna hands   I presume she had moved on to
another house or mistress, for I awaited and never received her
replies   One letter I handcopied forty times and sent to forty
capitals of the world   I offered her the fare, her own room in my
home   I promised sons to her*

   *λ You have come to me via three Harappas still desiring her*

*The citizens you met along the way were mute with desire, had lost the words to even state their wants   In time you will be with her   You once believed that abstinence and silence would witch you flight by the right of name and birth   You read of charms and chants in an ancient book   You sought to search forty capitals for your lover   I have one gift for you, Manu, but it is not flight*  λ



δ



λ *There was a fourth Harappa that you didn't reach   I took your boat from a forgotten dream and left it to bear you toward the final Harappa*  λ

*I saw only the roofs of houses, branches poking from the tide of the broken river as I approached the outskirts of the fourth Harappa   I could have touched the steeplecross of a church, and further along my bow was splintered by a spiked iron gate   Gradually the force and depth of water decreased   I saw into windows of houses, walked through a hockey pitch where the moon's reflection trembled in every puddle   I came to a wall of sandbags, wading the last mile down a marketstreet   Dank citizens stood outside a library   I realised that I had not entered the fourth Harappa but I had met its citizens who had come to meet and bag the river   No one answered my questions   I dragged the boat to the library pillars, and left it along with other boats, canoes, rafts and dinghies   I walked inside*

*In a vellum-bound book a man was listing the names of family members   First names last   He sat at a table in front of a queue of people in oilcloths   Men emptied the brims of their*

hats   Many of the women, the children were barefoot with arms slung over each other   Cups of soup were passed along the queue   People exhaled steam after every sip   Their pockets bulged with bread   The library smelt of wet ash

The children seemed dumbstruck by the full push of river   Someone talked of a boy hanging pendulous on a tyreswing above the rushing water   Others talked of the floods of '36, of '44   Someone screamed as water leaked through the wall of sand   People jostled at the library doors   Some raced to add more bags   Others ran

Eight naked men appeared at the wall of sand   The rainfall increased   The citizens fell down on their knees at the sight of the men   The naked men stroked their penises   Then with their penises erect the men began to dance with water rising to their ankles   Their hands mimed rain and then their arms spread-eagled and their fingertips twitched like the corona of the sun   One man ejaculated and left the dance and a citizen came and covered him with fistfuls of clay   Throughout they kept an equal distance between their bodies, even as they fell and rolled, even as they strung their invisible bows and became the seven invisible arrows aimed at the sky   The bodies of the remaining seven dancers began to jerk and spasm, so a few slowed and curved their spines and one dancer bit his arm   Then one by one the men ejaculated onto the ground and the citizens looked upward   For a long time everyone stood still in the rain   Then the dancers one by one stood up and mimed arrows falling to the earth

I am undaunted by water   I have lived and died by it

I left the dancers and the citizens and found the boy with his shoebox sitting in the boat   He was dressed in a cloak but I *knew it to be him He was the same height as when I met him but looked thinner I asked him why he hadn't returned to us, when my lover and I were good to him, when we fed him with food we were saving for ourselves He did not turn around He began to row but somewhere, somehow he took the boat and left me, for I arrived into this clay house on foot*

δ

λ *I have for you this barter, Manu, your hands for words Other men have lines of life and love upon their palms, Manu, but yours are without lines Once your lover held them to her eyes and saw the full absence of you I will place your hands over your eyes and you will look deep into the hollows and you will enter where I cannot enter, the fourth Harappa, and you will surrender all your words* λ

*I am rowing toward a grotto shaped like the plastron of a turtle A grotto encircles the woman Her eyes appear above the blue border of veil Her shadows are drawn upon with henna I want to hold her in my hands, hold her hands She bears me to a hotel where ivy hangs from marble pillars I am brushed by shoulders invisible and smell the breaths of mouths unseen I follow her along a hallway where polished black leather shoes are laid out before each door She opens a door to a room where a feast is laid A bed faces the window She unravels the veil of sheets The windows are sheathed in a fine and intricate embroidery of feathers I stand at the window and look out at the confluence of rivers The river holds the stars, inverts Orion She begins to sort the stars*

*I unscrew the window stained with memory and dream
The glass retains its rectangle of river and sky   The boy falls
from the sky, from Amba; the sky from Amba   I am deep into
the river   I am diving after the sky, diving   Amba wears a
dress of henna, of fire, down into the wet sky of fire   I am reaching her, past her, reaching past her for a chain of evil stars   The
diamond fires the coal fires of the earthstars and reaching past
for the river laced with gold   I am reaching with my hands over
my eyes*

φ

Something began to puzzle me. In legends of *Kṛṣṇa* I found neither rivers nor a single lover. He had multiplied to seduce a group of milkherds and certainly had cavorted with the gods, but there was nowhere the mention of one true earthly love by the confluence of rivers. I found his consort Radha but thought her more a cosmic entity than a woman and I failed to find any illustration of her leading a peacock or wearing bracelets upon her arms. I felt sure then of my earlier intimation, that the weaver had paired a god and woman across the histories, across the legends of the world, and it seemed to me that around the lover had been woven a disguise of centuries, of customs I could not unravel.

I have often imagined that when a man awakes and dresses in the morning he wraps around his soul a cloak. I imagined women dressing their souls in scarves of silk, painting their souls with henna. I imagined that even if I possessed the sight to see within the souls of men and women I would find only a disguise or veil, and be always once removed from the truth I could not imagine or understand. Yet again, it seemed, I was at one remove from the truth of the partner.

δ

*My henna palms without lines of confluent skies   I am neither drowning on air breathing here breathing fire with the mouth within my palms nor there*

δ

I stopped waiting for Mirren when she was absent from the last parade. I had no clear reason for expecting her return amongst the revellers or the paraders but I believed I would glimpse her face or see a hand beckoning me down a moonlit alley and, following, find her. That same week in the city square I saw a man who from a soapbox foretold of the second brilliant falling of Christ unto the earth. I remembered the man from my childhood and realised that his message, his waiting, had remained unchanged and unsettled for a score of years. I resolved then, after I had listened in vain for the key in the door and footfalls on the stairs, after I had misheard my name called in the street and put my hand on the shoulders of a dozen red-haired girls, to allow Mirren her absence. I decided that a glimpse in dreams would one day be enough.

δ

*I take the boat from the river dre8am and row out onto the wovenriver   On the banks of the dr8eam dre8am the parapets and turrets of a temple are visible from the bracelets of the woman's arms   Her rivers are thought with henna   Her rivers are flowing with thighs   I chance upon a tributary of her bloodline   I dre8am flood*

δ

Yet I have never truly relinquished my quest for *Kṛṣṇa*'s lover. I have tried to look into the weaver's mind, the weaver's soul, and have sought her fabrication in further texts, in further lore. I read recently an archaeological text which proposed that ancient cultures founded myths upon the fossils they unearthed. I thought that the myth of Varuna might have been inspired by the remains of a pterodactyl, that a man buried upon a horse might have led to dreams of centaurs. I daydreamed of astronomers seeing in the sky the shapes of animals who had once trod the earth but who now lay deep beneath, and gods with arrows drawn for the hearts of dragons.

δ

*I cawking then   She taking the ink of me   Falling around the feathers summed exit into my mouth2   Having been gluts on the mares of her, enclosed in her sails   I mantle   She sa8cre*

δ

I imagined that if I could preserve my dreams, a young archaeologist a millennium from now would find in the silt of a riverbed the remains of a dream where a man pursued the sun. The sun would be depicted as a woman with flaming hair, her breasts thumbprinted from ochre. The man would be aboard a boat, forlorn at the loss of his lover. The find would set the archaeologist dreaming of a legend where a man had flown in pursuit of a woman he had loved, and the archaeologist would deduct that in an ancient city during times of eclipse, the näive citizens believed the sun had fled and only the flight of a lover could return it.

φ

λ *Infinity wax* λ

# Acknowledgments

Thanks to Harper & Row Publishers Inc. for use of 'Bifocal' from *Stories That Could Be True* by William Stafford, 1960. Thanks to Penguin Publishing Australia for publishing a section of this novel in *Hot Type*, 1995. A section of the novel was also published in *Picador New Writing 4*, 1997, edited by Beth Yahp and Nicolas Jose.

Many texts were consulted during the composing of this novel and though I cannot list all of them here I will acknowledge the following as being critical to the ideas behind the prose of this work: *The Women's Encyclopedia of Myths And Secrets* by Barbara G. Walker, HarperCollins, 1983; *The History of Ancient Geography* by Oliver. J. Thomsen, New York: Biblio and Tannen, 1965; *The Hero with a Thousand Faces* by Joseph Campbell, Abacus, 1975; *Jesus The Magician* by Morton Smith, Harper & Row, 1978; *The Illustrated Golden Bough* by Sir James George Frazer, Simon & Schuster, 1996; *Brewer's Dictionary of Phrase and Fable* Fifteenth Edition, Cassell, 1996; *The Observer's Book of Astronomy* by Patrick Moore, Frederick Warne & Co. Ltd, 1962.

Reader, please note that the world in which you read and the world of this work of fiction do not align. Any inclination to align them will only end in tears.

I would also like to acknowledge that two sections of this novel are rewritings. The section on Cortes was written *after* the essay 'The Passing Wisdom of Birds' in Barry

Lopez's *Crossing Open Ground*, Picador, 1988. The sentence concerning Mirren and the word 'love' was written after a Hemingway quote which I have only read/found as the epigraph to Gerald Murnane's novel *Inland*, Heinemann, 1992.

I must thank my parents Noel and Priscilla for their positive concern and love and my sister Deborah and cousin Ajai for financial and emotional support. Also my love flies to Jan and Rebecca Curran who assisted me at various stages and especially to Bob Curran who helped with research into astronomy, physics, Thoreau and who also held my hockey stick back from the face of my computer. 0–4.

Thanks to Lyn and Arrabella for guidance. Thankyou to Karen Ward and Annette Barlow and the staff at Allen & Unwin for their professionalism and all round sweetness.

To Sophie and Meredith, my attending angels, I offer cornflowers for holding my hand.

Woof, woof, woof, woof to Falstaff, Paul and Helen. Thankyou to Judith and Gerald.

And finally to my girls Melissa and Emily in whose eyes I find the dark poetry to live by and without—I dare not imagine without.

'M. Delhi. Sept. '94. Christopher.' ALWAYS